WILD
LIFE

ISBN: 978-0-9888433-4-9

WILD LIFE

BY

JEFF MENAPACE

MIND MESS PRESS

2015

CHAPTER 1

SOUTH FLORIDA
DEEP IN THE EVERGLADES

Travis always stopped to look at Uncle Harlon's gator farm before he went inside. Today, the boy hurried across the wooden bridge and towards his front door without so much as a pause for the impressive congregation of alligators around back.

The screen door flew open. Travis Roy appeared, battered and panting. The boy's grandmother was first to her feet, his mother shortly after, her belly of eight months slowing ascent.

"And now just what the hell is this?" Ida Roy took hold of her grandson's face by the jaw. Her hand, wrinkled and twisted by elements of time and labor, was not gentle as it turned the boy's head left and right to gauge the extent of his injuries. "Who done this to ya?"

Travis started to cry. His grandmother slapped him. "*Who done this to ya?*"

Travis looked over at his mother who now stood at his grandmother's side. Her face was as unyielding as his grandmother's. The audacity to cry from pain. There was no sympathy in this room for the boy. He'd been a fool to think otherwise.

Jolene Roy stepped forward and raised the back of her hand in threat. "You answer your meemaw. And you can go on and knock off that crying 'fore someone sees. Shameful enough we seen."

Travis straightened up and sniffed away the last of his tears. "Noah Daigle done it."

Ida grabbed her grandson's right hand and raised it to the thick lenses on the end of her nose. She turned the boy's hand over, inspecting the knuckles. "Not a bruise, not a scrape. Didn't get one lick in, did you? And I don't bother looking at your left; didn't get no licks in with your right, sure as shit didn't get none in with your left."

"Hit me when I wasn't looking," Travis pleaded.

"And put you clean out, did he?" Jolene Roy asked her son.

Travis shook his head emphatically with what little pride he had left. "Huh-uh. No, Mama, no. I didn't go out, I didn't go out."

Jolene made a face as if she meant to spit. "So you was fixed to keep fightin' then…"

The boy visibly deflated. He looked away and began fingering the gator tooth hanging from his neck, a pacifying habit during times of stress.

Ida Roy exchanged looks with her daughter-in-law, clucked her tongue and shook her head in disgust. "A Roy rolling over and taking a beating from a Daigle. *Not one damn swipe given back.*"

"Might have done if it'd just been Noah," the boy muttered, thumb and index finger still working on the tooth.

Jolene stepped forward. "*Say again!?*"

Travis steeled himself for what was to come. Talking back would guarantee a hiding far greater than the likes of Noah Daigle could ever dish out. But no hiding did come. His mother's eagerness for her son to repeat his mutterings was not rhetorical; was not the typical rumble of thunder before the crack. It was an atypical demand for elaboration, because Jolene Roy's genuine look of disbelief appeared as if she'd just heard the impossible.

And Travis suddenly knew why. And all at once he wanted to bonk his own head for not coming up with the lie sooner.

Louder, and with less shame, Travis said: "Might have done if it'd been just Noah."

Yes, the look his mother and grandmother now exchanged meant no hiding was on its way. A wicked little smile itched on the boy's face, and he dropped his head in case he lost the fight to contain it.

"You saying Noah Daigle wasn't the only one that done this?" Jolene asked her son.

Travis nodded, head still down. Talking into his chest, he said, "Noah and Ethan done it."

Ida Roy grabbed her grandson's face and jerked it upward, her bony fingers digging into his cheeks. The pain erased the itch for a smile. "You saying Ethan Daigle done it too? Wasn't no fair fight?"

Travis stared into his grandmother's eyes, saw the frightening potential staring back, her thick lenses enhancing a simmering rage that was all but spilling over and hissing on the fire…and Travis instantly regretted the lie.

You don't disrespect a Roy. Everyone knew that.

Ida gripped her grandson's cheeks tighter, brought her face to his. Breath as foul as the tobacco teeth before it shot into Travis' face. Ida's oral decay was not something she hid; it was wielded often like a bully's fist. "*You saying Ethan Daigle done it too? Wasn't no fair fight?*" she said again.

No going back now. Travis had thought himself a dummy for not conjuring the lie sooner, saving himself a hiding, saving himself the shame. He'd then flip-flopped the moment his grandmother latched onto his face, thought himself an even bigger dummy for lacking the foresight to know what would happen to the Daigles once he'd sold his lie. God might be able to forgive stealing a peek at Daddy's Playboys, or trying a swig of Uncle Harlon's whiskey, but a lie that would bring what his family would assuredly bring down upon the Daigles? He'd burn for it. Burn good and proper for all eternity.

He could take it all back, of course.

Admit that it *had* been a fair fight.

Admit that Ethan Daigle *hadn't* been involved.

Admit that he'd lied to his mama and meemaw.

Travis shuddered. The lie was now truth as far as he was concerned.

"No, Meemaw—wasn't no fair fight."

Ida let go of her grandson's face, gave it an apologetic wipe that contradicted the hate etched into the permanent frown lines of her brow. She glanced over at her daughter-in-law. "You go and you make this right, Jolene."

Jolene rubbed her full belly with both hands. "Better I don't wait for Tucker to come home first?"

Ida ignored her and marched towards the screen door, flinging it open with a bang that made Travis wince. She returned moments later, a rock the size of a softball in both hands. Went to the kitchen and snatched a large towel. Wrapped the rock in the towel until the weighted end hung from her knotted fist. A crude ball and chain.

She handed the makeshift weapon to Jolene and then gestured towards Travis. "You take your boy and you make it right"—Travis stood gaping, fingers working nervously on the gator tooth again—"you make him the angel that brings the righteous. You make him do it right."

Jolene measured the weight of the rock and towel, glanced over at Travis, then back at her mother-in-law. "Suppose they don't see it eye for an eye? Suppose they see fit to stopping us? Better I wait for Tucker?"

Ida snorted, her daughter-in-law's notion seemingly ludicrous. "They don't dare. *Nobody* dares touch a Roy when they're in the wrong—" A sinister little smile creased the corner of her leathery mouth. "Hell, even when they're in the right."

CHAPTER 2

Noah Daigle sat on the front porch next to his father, a pile of flat stones between them. They took turns skipping them into the river as they spoke.

"Put a proper one on him, did you?" Ron Daigle asked his son.

"Good and proper, Daddy."

Ron Daigle went to skip another stone but froze, arm in mid-air as he eyed his son. "And he had it coming? Wasn't your doing that started it up?"

"No, Daddy. I didn't wanna fight. He was the one that kept pushing. It was fair and proper."

Ron finally skipped his stone. He didn't appear relieved. "Yeah…them Roys though, you know how they get. They don't see fair and proper like others do."

Noah frowned and looked up at his father. "You mean they'd cause a fuss over a fair fight? One I wasn't even fixin' to start?"

Ron skipped another stone and sighed. "Ahh…you never can tell. That Harlon and Tucker Roy, they ain't the type that like losing. Harlon especially."

"Harlon Roy let me come along and watch him transport some gators to a watching spot up the river one time. He seemed nice enough."

Ron glanced over at his son. "It don't take much effort to *seem*, son. Even the devil can seem your friend...'til he gets his hooks in you. I seen Harlon Roy at his worst."

"What'd you see, Daddy?"

Ron shook his head. "Nothing your thirteen-year-old ears need hearing."

Noah moaned. And then a thought popped excitement into his eyes. "*You seen how he lost his leg?*"

Ron chuckled. "No. Story goes one of his own gators got that."

Noah looked disappointed. "Yeah, everyone knows that..."

Ron chuckled again. "So then why're you asking?"

"It's like you say about seeming. Not everything is like it seems. I reckon maybe he lost it another way, especially he's like you say he is."

"What, you think someone been wronged by Harlon come back one day and cut it off?"

"Sure, why not?"

Ron skipped a stone. "Because if someone was able to get through Harlon and Tucker, they sure as *heck* never getting through Ida Roy."

"Travis' mama?"

"Travis' *mee*maw. Mean old lady. Meaner than Harlon."

"I seen her," Noah said. "She keeps to their porch mostly, but I seen her. Looks like some swamp witch drift in from Louisiana."

Ron laughed, palmed his son's head and shoved it away playfully. "Sounds about right to me."

Noah skipped the last stone. It hit the water and jumped three times, settling and sinking a few feet from an approaching paddle boat. Travis Roy was rowing, his head down. His mother Jolene Roy sat at the bow, her head high, fixed on the approaching Daigle place. She did not look pleased.

CHAPTER 3

Ron Daigle made his way down the short dock from his porch. Noah followed his father.

"Jolene—" Ron said, gesturing towards the boat. "You think that's wise in your condition? Suppose you tip?"

Jolene didn't respond. Ron's courtesies only incensed her further, a coward's attempt at deflecting the issue at hand. *He* knew why she was there.

Travis Roy, head still down and unable to face the scene he'd created, docked the boat by the side of the river, and then helped his mother onto dry land. The two headed up the short ramp that connected to the Daigle's bridge, Jolene leading the way. The rock and towel swayed in her fist as she marched forward. Ron Daigle fixed on the swaying weapon, then back up at Jolene. There was fear in his eyes.

"What's this about, Jolene?"

"You know damn well what this is about, Ron Daigle." She pointed over his shoulder, towards Noah. "And if you don't, maybe you go and ask that little bastard of yours why we're here."

Ron raised a hand. "Whoa, now calm down, Jolene—you're outta line talking about my boy like that."

Jolene stepped forward, poked Roy hard in the chest. "You're outta line defending him when you know what he done!"

Ron took a step back. "This about the fight with him and Travis?"

"Wasn't no fight. Lessen you call two against one a fair fight. Needed the help of his big brother to get the job done!"

Ron turned his head slightly, keeping an eye on Jolene while he called back to his son. "What's she on about, Noah? You said it was a fair fight."

Noah stepped forward. "It *was*! Ethan wasn't involved."

Jolene gestured back towards Travis. "My boy says otherwise. Look at the state of him. Ain't no one boy doing that to a Roy."

Ron leaned to one side and studied Travis' beaten face. Travis refused to meet his gaze. "You sayin' Noah *and* Ethan done that to you, Travis?" Ron asked.

Travis nodded, still refusing eye contact, fingers working vigorously on the gator tooth around his neck as if he meant to whittle it down to nothing.

Noah took an adamant stomp forward, joining his father's side. "You're a liar, Travis Roy! It was a fair and proper fight. Ethan wasn't involved!"

Jolene shoved Noah back a step. Ron stepped in front of his son to shield him. "Now come on, Jolene…"

"That little bastard of yours is calling my boy a liar! Wasn't no fair fight. But we come now to settle things. Take what's ours."

Ron started backing away, reaching behind and nudging his son along with him, eyes shifting back and forth between Jolene's unyielding gaze and the weapon dangling at her side. "Now, Jolene, you just wait a minute…no one's calling nobody nuthin. I ain't seen Ethan all day, and that's the God's honest truth. My boy tells me it was a fair and proper fight, and I believe him."

Jolene stepped forward. "So now you're calling my boy a liar too?"

"I just told you, Jolene; no one's calling nobody nuthin. I'm just saying I believe my boy."

Her eyes narrowed. "And I'm saying I believe *mine.* We gotta make this right, Ron Daigle, lessen you want Tucker and Harlon coming down here to sort things."

The blood drained from Ron's face. "Now come on, Jolene…"

"*Come on, Jolene* nuthin. We're gonna make this right, Ron Daigle. Here and now."

A screen door banged behind Ron and Noah. Jolene Roy cocked her head to one side to get a look. Ron and Noah did not risk taking their eyes off Jolene.

"Here, what's this?"

"Go back inside, Adelyn," Ron called over his shoulder.

Adelyn Daigle stayed put. "Jolene Roy, what're you doing here in your condition? You're looking fixed to pop, girl."

"Here to teach your boy a thing or two about what happens when you cross a Roy. Wouldn't think you Daigles needed such a lesson, Adelyn."

Adelyn frowned. "What's she on about, Ron? This about the fight between our Noah and her Travis?"

"It's about the fight between my Travis, your Noah, *and your Ethan.*"

Surprise inverted the v of Adelyn's frown. "Ethan? Ethan wasn't involved, Jolene. It was a fair fight."

"And you seen this with your own eyes, Adelyn?" Jolene said.

"Well, no…but Noah said—"

"'*Noah said!*'" Jolene blurted. "Well, *my boy said* your Ethan *was* involved. That's enough for me. Now both of you tell your Noah to come forward so we can make this right. I already told Ron he don't want Tucker and Harlon coming down here to see to it, Adelyn. And I imagine you agree. Now, you tell your Noah to step forward."

Noah wormed around his father, confronted Jolene. "I ain't done nuthin! Was a fair fight!" Desperate tears filled his eyes. "*Your boy's a damn liar!*"

The sound of Jolene Roy slapping Noah Daigle was like a whip cracking. The boy staggered, fear and anger wiped clean off his face. What remained was a fitting portrait of shock.

Adelyn Daigle rushed forward. Jolene Roy pointed a finger at her and commanded she stay put. Adelyn froze as if Jolene's finger were a gun.

Ron Daigle stayed reluctantly fixed to his spot, anger fighting common sense. He did not
want a war with the Roys.

Jolene glanced over her shoulder. "Travis, get over here."

Travis approached sheepishly. Jolene presented her son with the rock and towel. "Now you go and take what's yours, Travis Roy."

Travis hesitated.

"Take it!"

Adelyn cried out. "Christ almighty, Jolene, can't you see the boy don't want it!? He *knows* this ain't right! Travis, tell her. Tell your mama my boys ain't done wrong by you! *Please!*"

Travis looked up at his mother. The look she cast back down on her son allowed no chance for salvation should he come clean. His choice was simple. Keep lying and forever carry the weight of what would come to Noah Daigle...or tell the truth and face what would come to him, from his own.

He chose Noah Daigle.

Travis took the rock and towel from his mother and started toward Noah.

Ron Daigle twitched.

Jolene thrust her finger. "You stay put, Ron Daigle. *God help you, if you don't.*"

Adelyn cried for her son.

Jolene thrust her finger on Adelyn now. "And you can shut that up right now, Adelyn! *Your* fault you done raised boys who don't know right from wrong." Her possessed gaze fell back on Travis. "*Well, go on!*"

Noah Daigle's shock from Jolene's blow had diffused. He was back to frightened tears as Travis approached. He did not offer up any means of defense, just stood still, bracing himself. "You're a damn liar, Travis Roy," he said, full-on crying now. "You're gonna burn come judgment."

Travis swung the weighted towel, the rock hitting Noah on the side of the head. The boy dropped instantly, unconscious. Adelyn screamed and instinctively rushed forward. Ron spun and stopped her charge, urging her back.

"Hit him again!" Jolene yelled.

Ron's head whipped back towards Jolene, eyes wide and incredulous. "*Again!?* Jolene, that's enough!"

Jolene ignored him. "Travis Roy, you hit him again!" Her possessed gaze then snapped onto Ron with righteous intent. "Was only supposed to be one each, but since you say Ethan ain't here to take his, I reckon Noah gets *two*!"

Ron finally moved. He stepped in front of his unconscious son, splayed both hands and stuck out his chest. "Hit *me* then. You say we're responsible for our boys, so go on and hit *me* then. I'm responsible. Go on, Travis, hit me."

Travis looked over at his mother, confused. Ron Daigle's plea only seemed to incense Jolene further. "You get the hell out of the way, Ron Daigle. I've been letting you slide with too many warnings as it is."

Tears of helpless rage started in Ron's eyes. He refused to blink them away, kept them wide and glassy and stuck on Jolene with unmovable conviction. "Your boy swings again and our Noah's gonna end up funny. Please, Jolene…"

"Boy's *already* funny thinking he could do what he done and get away with it." Back to her son: "Travis Roy, goddammit, I ain't gonna tell you again."

Ron looked hard at Travis. "Travis, don't do it. Whatever went down between you and Noah don't justify this. You *know* that, son. You and Noah, you played together when you were little. *Please*, Travis, don't do this…"

Travis dropped his head, the towel and rock in his right hand dropping to his side where it hung in a limp dangle.

Jolene snatched the weapon from her son. "You just wait until your daddy hears about this, Travis Roy. Lord have mercy, you just wait..."

Jolene readied the towel and rock in her right fist, went to step around Ron Daigle to get to Noah's unconscious body. Ron blocked her path. "I can't let you do it, Jolene!"

Jolene swung the rock and towel at Ron's head. Ron blocked the swing with his forearm and grabbed Jolene's shoulders. They grappled upright, twirling around in a fevered embrace, Jolene desperately trying to swing the rock and towel, Ron desperately trying to defend without harming the woman and her unborn child, constantly screaming *"Jolene, stop! Jolene, stop! Jolene, stop!"*

Jolene took one last swing. Ron ducked under the blow and Jolene pitched herself over the side of the bridge's rail, landing in a shallow pool of swamp water, her head cracking one of few sizeable rocks jutting out from beneath, body going rigid, seizing up before it went slack and lay face down in the shallow green water. No air bubbles surfaced around her head.

"*MAMA!*" Travis cried, now leaning over the railing, gaping down at his mother's body. "*MAMA!*" he cried again, throwing himself over the railing, landing and then stumbling face-first into the shallows. He surfaced with a panicked gasp and hurried towards his mother. Rolled her over. Jolene Roy's forehead was concaved, the deepest part of the depression split and pumping a dark red into the surrounding green water, turning it brown. "*MAMA!*" He shook her repeatedly. Her eyes would not blink.

"*Travis!*"

Travis looked up and behind him. Ron Daigle hung over the bridge's rail, his face lost; his cry of the boy's name more reflex than the start of any definitive action.

Travis spun and hurried towards his boat, leaving his mother's body.

"*Travis!*" Ron sprinted down the dock, hoping to meet the boy where land and bridge came together. Travis arrived first and jumped into the boat, readying the oars, pushing off. Ron arrived seconds after, wading into the river, reaching for the boat's edge. *"Travis, wait!"* Travis swung one of the oars and caught Ron behind the ear, shaking his consciousness, causing him to stumble and fall back into the water.

By the time Ron was able to stand and clear his head, Travis was squinting distance down the river, assuredly on his way home to tell his family what had happened.

Ron turned and trudged through the shallows. Headed up the ramp and then across the bridge to see to his wife and son. Noah was coming to. Adelyn cradled him in both arms, but her eyes were on her approaching husband. She did not look sad or remorseful. She looked terrified. "Ron Daigle," she said, "what have we done?"

CHAPTER 4

SOUTHWEST FLORIDA INTERNATIONAL AIRPORT
FORT MYERS, FLORIDA

Elizabeth Burk spotted her parents in the distance. "There they are," she said, and began waving an arm.

Dan Rolston, sizeable bag slung over one shoulder, stopped for a second and stood on his toes to try and get a good look at his girlfriend's folks. Up until now, he'd only seen pictures.

He saw a couple waving back with big smiles. They looked as they did in the photographs he'd seen. Tan, attractive, what appeared to be genuinely happy people. Photos could lie of course, but then Elizabeth had been a treasured find. The rare mix of beautiful and good. Not a bad bone in her body, unless they were in the bedroom that is, bless her heart. If the Burks were even *half* as decent as the job they'd done raising Elizabeth, they were just fine in Dan's book.

Elizabeth, pace quickening at the excitement of seeing her mom and dad for the first time in six months, gave Dan a quick glance over her shoulder. "Nervous?"

They were getting closer. Twenty yards tops. "Do I go in for the hug?" Dan asked.

"Do whatever feels natural."

"Fist bump then."

She laughed. "And for my mom?"

"Open-mouth kiss."

"Eww."

Ten yards...

Elizabeth started waving again, the smile on her face spreading into an eager grin. Dan waved and smiled too. It felt weird, like waving to an acquaintance who, upon deeper scrutiny, turned out to be a complete stranger.

"Tell me again why they'll love me," he said out of the side of his mouth.

"Because *I* love you," she responded from the side of hers.

"Not good enough."

Five yards...

They carried on like amateur ventriloquists.

"Honey, they're gonna love you. My mom loves your books."

"But your dad hates them."

"He hates your *genre*. He's a fraidy cat. At least he still read some."

Dan nodded. "True."

Touchdown.

Elizabeth got a dual hug and kiss from mom and dad, and then came the moment of truth. All three turned and faced Dan.

"Mom? Dad? This is Dan."

Dan started with Mrs. Burk. He chose to go in for the hug, and her extended hand caught him in the chest. Dan backed up, blushed, gave an awkward laugh, and extended his hand... which in turn caught *her* in the chest—right smack on a boob—as she went in to accommodate his wish for a hug.

Dan was purple now. Out of his mouth like a hiccup, he said: "Ah shit."

A moment of silence. Dan contemplated charging airport security in hopes of getting shot. And then Russ and Vicky Burk burst out laughing, Vicky Burk grabbing hold of Dan's face, planting one on his cheek, then turning to Elizabeth and saying, "Oh, I like him already. Will be nice to tell the girls at the club a young man tried to cop a feel."

Dan, no less purple, chuckled along. He still wanted to crawl into a hole.

"You only get one of those, you know," Russ Burk said, waving a playful fist at Dan.

Dan chuckled again, and reluctantly offered his hand once more lest he feel up Elizabeth's dad too. Russ took it with a big smile, adding several friendly pats on Dan's shoulder as he did so, each pat more cathartic than the last.

Yup. Genuinely happy people. More importantly, genuinely *cool* people. Dan's face was back to its original color in no time.

CHAPTER 5

Ron Daigle stood on his front porch, shotgun ready, his boys Noah and Ethan flanking him, both armed with a 30-30 Winchester rifle. Adelyn Daigle sat behind her husband and sons, rocking nervously in her chair, eyes stuck on the river ahead, and whatever that river might bring.

Noah Daigle broke the long silence. "You believe us, don't you, Daddy? Ethan not being involved and all? You believe Travis and me had a fair fight?"

Ron Daigle kept his eyes on the river as he answered. "I believe you, son. But I don't reckon it matters much now, do you?"

Noah dropped his head and shook it.

Ron and Ethan had lifted Jolene Roy's corpse from the water and carried it into their home where it still lay with a green table cloth covering it. For the several hours it lay on the floor, not one family member could bring themselves to look at it.

"I still reckon we call the sheriff," Ethan said. "Connor James can vouch for my whereabouts when Noah and Travis had their fight. They can see the Roys were in the wrong. What happened after that was their own doing."

Ron gave his son a somber, sidelong glance. "You reckon the sheriff's gonna get mixed up in some Roy business, do you, son?"

Ethan spun and hollered into the riverbank's dense forest beyond. "*Bullshit* is what it is!"

"Ethan Daigle!" Adelyn scolded from her chair.

Ethan turned back to his father, gripping the Winchester tight to his chest. "So what're we supposed to do then? Stand her 'til Lord knows how long, waiting for a comeuppance we don't deserve?"

Ron looked back out onto the river, a deep sadness falling over his face. "I don't know, son. I only know the sheriff won't be getting involved. I know them Roys will be coming for us—" Ron spit into the river, his sadness changing to a helpless disgust. "And I know they'll be fixin' to get nasty when it comes to that comeuppance we don't deserve."

CHAPTER 6

Russ Burk drove his new Lexus south along Interstate 75 towards Bonita Springs. Vicky rode in the passenger seat, Elizabeth and Dan in back.

"You haven't been in the new car yet, have you, Liz?" Russ said over his shoulder.

"No—first time. It's nice, Dad." She turned to Dan, smiled, and then squeezed his hand. He smiled back and squeezed longer than she had—a reassuring squeeze.

Dan already knew Elizabeth's parents were well off; she'd told him a few times, almost *warning* Dan as her love for him grew. Sad as it may seem, Elizabeth felt a family with money was something to be kept close to the chest for fear of the negative stereotypes often administered to the wealthy before hello one had even been uttered. Dan was different of course, but still, there would always be that concern. Especially when they would arrive at Bonita Springs and Dan would see the Burks' place, and just how deep that vein of wealth ran.

"This isn't your first time to Florida, is it, Dan?" Vicky asked.

Dan sat up in his seat. "Uh, no—I was in Clearwater a few years back."

"Love Clearwater," Vicky said. "Beautiful."

"Yeah, it was."

"When are we taking him to Disney?" Russ asked his daughter, a sly smile on his profile while he kept his eyes on the road.

"Oh geez—I don't think he's ready for that yet, Dad." Elizabeth turned to Dan. "My family is *obsessed* with Disneyworld."

"You ever been, Dan?" Russ asked.

Again the upright attention in his seat. "Uh, no, Russ. I guess I'm not really a Disney fan."

Vicky turned in her seat and slapped a hand to her chest, mouth falling open in mock shock. "*Not a Disney fan?* Oh, Elizabeth, how are we going to fix this?"

Russ reached behind his seat, gesturing for Dan's hand. "Finally! An ally."

Dan happily took Russ' hand and shook it.

"Oh, shut up, Dad; you love Disney."

"I love it because you guys love it."

"He's trying to act macho for you, Dan," Vicky said. "Don't listen to him."

Russ smiled and shook his head in defeat.

"No worries, Russ," Dan said. "If we ever go, you and I can feign happiness together."

"It *is* the happiest place on Earth," Vicky said.

Dan groaned, and everyone laughed. Dan was getting a pleasant vibe, feeling more and more at ease.

"So, Dan," Russ began, "how are book sales going?"

Ah yes, the *can you provide for our daughter, should the time come?* query. He'd expected it.

"Good, not great," Dan said. "I have a nice little following."

Elizabeth broke in. "He has a *great* following. He's always getting emails from fans."

Dan didn't interject. As an indie author who busted his ass with everything from the book content itself, to cover design, to freelance editors, and to the almighty dread that is self-marketing, he was happy to hear the praise, even if it was from his girlfriend.

"Well, I *love* your stuff," Vicky said.

"You've read my work?" Dan asked, knowing she had.

Elizabeth said, and none too softly, "I told you she has."

"Oh right." His play at casual indifference was stuffed handily, Elizabeth lead tackle.

"She really does though," Elizabeth said. "You've read them all, right, Mom?"

This, Dan did not know. To date, he'd released five novels, two of them good earners, the remaining three decent. Critical reception was similar: good to decent; ironically, the modest earners receiving the bulk of that good praise, while his top earner absorbed plenty of hefty thumps. It was a mystery he would never understand, nor want to drive himself nuts by trying. Still, he had not known Elizabeth's mom had read *all five*.

"You read *all* of my books?" he asked.

"I did," Vicky said.

"Wow—I'm flattered. Thank you."

Vicky turned in her seat and made eye contact. "I really did like them a lot. And I'm not trying to win you over."

"Really?" Dan said. "Because I'm trying desperately."

Another group chuckle in the car.

"Dare I ask you what you thought, Russ?" Dan asked.

"I thought the writing was very good," Russ said.

"*Buuut…?*" Dan sang, studying Russ and Vicky's profiles after his risky cast. They were both smiling accordingly, and he was again grateful for their reception to his chanced wit.

"*Buuut*…my dad is a big sissy," Elizabeth said.

Profile still smiling, Russ could only nod. "It's true—I admit it."

"Hey, at least you read them," Dan said. "Elizabeth told me you're a history buff. I'd need a gun to my head to read the stuff you do."

Vicky raised her hand. "Gun for me too."

Dan looked at Elizabeth, and, casting another risky line loud enough for all to hear, said: "I think I may know who my favorite is, honey."

Another group chuckle. He was being himself and they liked it. Awesome.

"So, right now you're working on a book that takes place in the Everglades?" Russ asked.

"Yes," Dan said. "It was going to take place in Louisiana with elements of voodoo and everything, but I didn't want to get any facts wrong when it came to representing the religion. I'll admit I'm a bit lazy when it comes to research."

"So how do you plan to research the Everglades while you're here?" Vicky asked.

"I was hoping Elizabeth and I could take a day trip and let some locals do all the work for me. They'll talk; I'll jot. Can't get any lazier than that."

They all smiled, but there was something brimming behind those smiles. A palpable eagerness.

"And that might be the *perfect* introduction..." Russ said.

"Come again?" Dan said.

Russ took his eyes off the road for a tick and glanced back at Elizabeth, his eager beaming ever present, urging her to take the floor.

Elizabeth turned to Dan with an excited grin. "My dad is taking us on a swamp tour tomorrow morning."

"The *best* swamp tour," Russ said, his own excitement demanding bells and whistles. "Vicky and I went last year. We've done a few, and this was absolutely the *best*. The tour guide takes you deep, deep into the Everglades and shows you the works."

"You're kidding me?" Dan said.

"Nope," Vicky said. "It was fantastic. Gators and pythons and—"

"*Pythons?*"

"Yup. Our guide pointed one out to us. We never would have spotted it otherwise. It was all coiled up and hidden in the vegetation along an embankment we were passing." Vicky made a frightened face and pretended to shiver. "It was *huge*."

"So that really is a thing, huh?" Dan asked. "The python problem down here I've been reading about? I read a few articles that said it was embellished and not the issue many claim it to be."

Dan was all too familiar with the current event of people purchasing baby Burmese pythons and then setting them free into the wild where they would mate like teens and reproduce like Irish Catholics. He had even planned on having a giant python attack and eat one of the protagonists in his story. Problem was, the more he dug, the more he found that the problem was overblown, a combination of fear-inducing media nonsense, and locals attracting crazy python-hunting tourists in a bid to make a few bucks.

The other problem was that while pythons had been known to attack people here and there, the attacks were usually aborted attempts at a meal. Once they went for a nibble and realized just what they'd have to swallow to gain that meal, an *Eff that* was the snake's typical response—adults, it would seem, were just too big to try and gulp.

He'd heard awful stories of pythons and the like crawling out of their cages and strangling children, but those sad exceptions were always attributed to human idiocy. Could such a thing happen to a child in the wild? Sure—it *could*, he supposed. Dan could try and make it happen on the written page. But how believable would it be to have a child wandering around the Everglades on foot to allow such gruesomeness to happen? And it would be gruesome. *Too* gruesome. Dan likened children being killed in books to politics and religion being discussed in a bar. Just don't.

There *had* been accounts of snakes attacking adults and carrying on with full intention of a meal—apparently if a snake was hungry enough, it would go after anything—but more often than not, the snake would choke to death on its own sizeable catch. Dan had seen a good number of images of dead pythons with antelope horns, deer hooves, or gator tails ripped through and jutting from their bloated bodies. Indigestion at its finest.

"I'm not too sure," Russ said. "That's something you can ask and jot tomorrow morning."

Dan smiled. Ask and jot he would. But hell, even if the tour guide confirmed his own research, Dan wasn't about to let the truth get in the way of a good story. He wanted a python to gobble somebody up in his new book. In fact, speaking of good stories...

"First, let me just say thank you so much," he said. "Really, this is such a kind gesture. It's going to help immensely." He thought about leaning forward and touching them both on the arm. Too much? Ah screw it, he'd already touched Vicky's boob. "Thank you," he said again, leaning forward and touching them both lightly on the shoulder. It came off natural, the couple smiled, and when Dan sat back, he saw that Elizabeth was smiling too.

"Second," he began, "let me tell you this snake story."

"*Oooh!*" Elizabeth broke in, "tell them the one your mom told us. About the snake in the woman's bed."

"I was just about to, Spoiler Alert."

Elizabeth slapped a hand over her mouth.

Russ laughed.

Dan smiled and squeezed Elizabeth's knee.

"What's the story?" Vicky asked.

"My mother was telling me about this woman she works with who, for whatever reason, had this huge pet python. Classic compensation for her boyfriend coming up short perhaps."

Another risky joke, but both Russ and Vicky laughed.

"Anyway, she had this huge python, and one day it stopped eating. Normally she would feed it a big rat every two to three weeks, but it simply wouldn't eat. Concerned, she takes it to the vet, and the vet says not to worry; pythons can go a long time without eating, and if this continues for a couple more weeks, bring it on back.

"So it continues, and she brings it back to the vet a couple of weeks later. The vet asks if the snake has exhibited any odd behavior, and the girl says as a matter of fact it has. She woke one morning to find the snake *in bed with her.* It had slithered out of its cage and gotten into her bed."

"Oh my God," Vicky said.

"I know," Elizabeth said. "Can you imagine?"

Dan went on. "Believe it or not, the girl didn't freak. She just picked the snake up and put it back in its tank. When the vet asked her if the snake had been coiled up next to her, perhaps seeking warmth, the woman said no; oddly enough, the snake had been lying straight, up and down the bed like a thick length of hose. The vet's immediate reply? The snake needs to be put down. Upset, the girl asks why, what's wrong with it? To which the vet replies that the snake had been intentionally starving itself in preparation for a meal far greater than a measly rat. By lying next to the woman, it was literally measuring to see if it would be able to swallow her."

"Oh my God," Vicky said again.

Dan smiled as if he'd just told a good joke. "How messed up is that?"

"Why on Earth would anyone have a pet like that?" Russ said.

"Preaching to the choir, Russ," Dan said. "I read an article about some idiots who put their baby in the same room as their pet python. Need I tell you what happened?"

"No," Vicky said adamantly.

"I don't get people sometimes," Russ said.

"At least the snake was just being a snake," Dan said. "What's the excuse for people like that?"

"No creature more frightening than man, stupidity not excluded," Russ said.

"Uh...I'd rather face a man than a giant snake, Dad," Elizabeth said.

"Yeah, but what Dan said is true. The snake was just being a snake. Humans are the only living things that cause pain by choice."

CHAPTER 7

Dusk.

Ron Daigle and his two boys hadn't moved from their front porch. Fear kept them alert. Only Adelyn Daigle exhibited signs of fatigue due to her seated position behind them.

"Perhaps they won't show?" Adelyn said.

Ron glanced back at his wife. "You believe that, Adelyn?"

"Maybe Travis explained it was an accident?"

Now Ron turned and faced his wife completely, shotgun at his side. "Boy lied about his fight with Noah. Now his mama's lying dead on our living room floor—her *and* her unborn child. All on account of his lie. If you think he's gonna start telling the truth now…"

Adelyn broke eye contact with her husband, fear coming back like a jolt of adrenaline. Ron nodded and turned back to the river. He squinted into the distance. Dusk was gaining strength.

"Go and hit the floodlights, Noah—" Ron said, looking east and then west into the dense wetlands lining both sides of the river. "Roys are crazy enough to try and come through on foot."

Noah went inside. A moment later, powerful bursts of light shot from the roof of the Daigle home, shining down and reflecting off the dark river. The sound of aquatic life, irritated by the new light, could be heard lightly splashing as it dove for cover. No heavy splashing that was cause for alarm.

The floodlights were strong, but not so strong that they penetrated the surrounding forest adequately. Maybe a few feet inward until the increasing dark reclaimed its hold. Ron leaned forward onto the rail of his porch, squinting and looking east and west again, desperate to spot something in what light penetrated the wetlands. He saw nothing. "Where are you sons of bitches," he murmured.

Noah reappeared, screen door banging behind him. "How's that, Daddy?"

Ron nodded but kept his gaze on the river and beyond. "That's good, son."

Ethan's fear was accompanied by his increasing agitation. "We planning to be out here all night, Daddy?" There was contempt in his voice.

"Better we go inside and let them surprise us?" Ron asked his son.

"No, but I'm not fixin' to sleep out here. I seen gators chance our bridge before. Black bear too."

"We'll sleep in shifts if we have to," Ron said.

Ethan turned his attention back to the river, muttered: "*Bullshit.*"

"I heard that, Ethan Daigle," Adelyn said. "The mouth on this one, Ron."

"Mind your mother," Ron said absently, his voice sounding far away.

Noah was the first to catch the bobbing light on the river. "Daddy!"

A row boat was approaching, a powerful flashlight its guide at the bow. As the bobbing circle of light grew, Ron could begin to make out the boat's occupants. Ida Roy was at the bow, flashlight in hand, pointing the powerful beam at the Daigle home with such hatred in her face it seemed as if she entertained the flashlight a ray of fire. Tucker Roy was rowing. There was no hatred on his face. It was granite. The face of a man who would not allow death to stop him.

Travis Roy was not in the boat. Neither was his uncle Harlon. While Ron saw no cause for alarm at Travis' absence, he took significant note of Harlon's. That man would have been first in line for a helping of vengeance.

The boat was a good ten feet from the Daigle's bridge when Ron fired the shotgun into the air. The blast echoed throughout their remote surroundings like an errant firework. Ron then pumped the shotgun—hard and demonstratively—and pointed it at the Roys. "That's far enough, Tucker."

Ida Roy spit over the side of the boat. "Not *nearly* far enough, Ron Daigle." Her voice, deep and rough like an old man's, made Ron flash on Noah's earlier reference to a witch. It was more fitting now than it'd ever been, and it clicked Ron's fear up a peg.

"I reckon Travis told you what happened," Ron said. "I only hope he spoke the truth this time; told you what happened was an accident." Calling Travis on his lying would only incite the Roys, but he had to project some measure of confidence, even if he felt little.

"We come for the body," Tucker Roy said. His face was as stone as ever, no affect at all. "You let us take Jolene home and give her a proper send off. You're a smart man, Ron. Don't make things worse than they already are."

Ron had expected this, but he wasn't about to let a Roy into his home. Even—hell, *especially*—Ida. "My boys will bring her out to you, Tucker. We'll lay her at the end of the dock. When we're back up here and safe, you can come forward and collect her."

Ida Roy spit again. "Listen to you talkin' like you're in the right."

"What happened was an accident, Ida. Your Jolene came here fixin' to ruin our Noah for life. We were only trying to stop it."

"You know what's coming, boy," Ida said. "You don't get it now, you'll get it soon enough."

Ron gripped the shotgun tight to his chest. "And we'll be waiting, Ida. You won't be hurting my family over an accident."

"An accident that woulda never been if it weren't for them little shits you call sons," Ida said.

Ethan burst forward. "I was never involved! Noah and Travis had a fair fight! This is all *your* doing!"

"*Ethan!*" Adelyn said from behind.

The hatred in Ida Roy's face leapt to a incredulous rage. "The cheek of that one! I reckon you tell him to shut his mouth before I do his tongue!"

Ron, eyes never leaving the boat, said: "You hush, Ethan, you hear me?"

Ethan said nothing.

"Fine group of boys you got there, Ron Daigle," Ida said. "A liar, and a disrespectful little shit. I reckon both will do just fine when it comes to feeding Harlon's flock."

Ron's fear scorched his throat, increasing his need to swallow nothing but his body's irony for that need. He fought the urge so they would not see him cough, blocking out any remaining windows into his fear. He steadied the gun and cleared his throat as quietly as he could. "You can go and knock that kinda talk off right now, Ida. You want to collect Jolene or don't you?"

Ida and Tucker exchanged looks.

"Tell your boys to bring my wife down then," Tucker said.

Tucker's demeanor bothered Ron. Tucker Roy was a hard man; Ron expected no tears or sadness. But he did not expect the measure of calm he was exhibiting. The hate was there, that was evident. But the control he was displaying in the face of such hate—Ron found it more worrisome than any of Ida Roy's threats.

"Alright then," Ron said. "You keep that boat right where it is for now." He turned left and then right, between his two boys. "Noah. Ethan. You boys go inside and see to Jolene." Then loud enough for the Roys to hear: "My boys will be bringing her down, Tucker. I'll be following right behind—" He brandished the shotgun. "If you've got any weapons hiding in that boat, I suggest you reconsider."

Ida Roy sneered. "Talkin' like you're in the right again…"

Ron ignored her. "Once we set Jolene down, and we're a safe distance back here, then you can come forward and collect her."

Ida Roy stood suddenly, rocking the boat. She pointed a finger at Ron. "*You don't tell us what's what!*" Her wretched voice cracked and she began a violent cough. When it passed, she said, "I swear to Christ on His throne, Ron Daigle, a suffering you never imagined is coming your way."

"Mama," Tucker said calmly. "Mama, please sit down." Ida reluctantly sat, venom leaking from her pores. Tucker looked up at the porch. "Bring her on down then, Ron. And you tell your boys to mind my wife."

Ron gave one emphatic nod. "Wouldn't have it any other way, Tucker." He turned left and right between Noah and Ethan again. "Go on, boys."

Ron felt no measure of relief from the understanding he and Tucker had just come to. The lion was in the room. It had promised to go away without bother once it had gotten what it came for. But Ron had lived in the wilderness long enough to know that anything wild could never be trusted.

Noah and Ethan had brought Jolene Roy's body to the edge of the Daigle's bridge, just as Ron had promised. And the boys were gentle and respectful as they laid her body, still covered in the green table cloth, to the wooden floor of the bridge, just as Ron had promised. And Ron had kept his shotgun aimed on the boat holding Ida and Tucker Roy the entire time, just as he'd promised.

His family back on their front porch without incident, Ron now called to the boat. "Alright, Tucker."

Tucker rowed towards the edge of the bridge, docking by the ramp. He whispered something to his mother, and then proceeded up the bridge towards his dead wife. His flat affect never changed, even when he squatted next to Jolene's body and pulled back the green table cloth to look at her lifeless face, and then pulling the table cloth down further, to her full belly, to his child that would never be.

And still, even after scooping his wife into his arms and then making his way down the bridge to lay her gently into the boat, Tucker Roy held no discernible expression of grief.

This was not the case for Ida Roy. A face that seldom expressed anything but contempt for the world now held the rare sight of sorrow as she ran a hand over her daughter-in-law's head. When the sorrow faded, and it had not stayed long, her gaze shifted back up towards the Daigles. Contempt had not returned. In its stead was a face of pure malevolence; and for the umpteenth time that day, Ron Daigle felt ice in his blood.

"Alright then, Tucker?" Ron called. But it was not alright. He knew that. He knew it would never be. His words were wishful projection, nothing more.

Tucker did not reply. He grabbed the oars and began rowing away. The lion was leaving the room. For now.

Ron called again: "Alright then, Tucker?"

Again, Tucker said nothing, just continued rowing. Odd as it may seem, Ron wanted them to stay, the anticipation of retribution far more crippling than the act itself. Whatever was to come, he wanted it now.

"Better we sort this now, Tucker?" He called to the departing boat, an almost pleading in his voice replacing all traces of bravado that may have been.

Ida Roy was the last to speak. "This is *not* alright, Ron Daigle. You know that. Once we see to Jolene, you've got a reckoning coming your way. Better you start teaching your family to sleep with both eyes open."

Ron opened his mouth to object—to *beg*—but the boat was moving steadily down the river now, and besides, even if Ron had the words, he knew it would only fuel their hate. To—and the sudden thought pumped a fresh supply of ice deeper into his veins—add to their delight when they sought fit to exact their revenge. Ron dropped his head in defeat and said nothing.

"Daddy?" Noah said. "Is it over now?"

Head still down, eyes closed, Ron said, "No, son." He eventually looked up and turned to Ethan. "Looks like we'll be sleeping in shifts after all." Then over his shoulder to his wife: "Better we go inside and get some supper. It's going to be a long night."

Adelyn nodded and stood.

"You boys go and help your mama with supper."

Ethan and Noah followed their mother inside.

Ron squinted out onto the river for a few minutes. He could no longer see the boat in the distance. They were gone. "But they'll be back," he whispered to himself. "Please, God Almighty, help us...they'll be back."

Ron sighed and went inside. There he found Harlon Roy standing behind Adelyn, a pistol pressed to her head. Noah and Ethan stood helpless nearby, hands in the air, their rifles discarded on the opposite side of the room.

"Evening, Ron," Harlon said. He took the gun off Adelyn's head and shot Ron in both legs, sending him to the ground in a writhing mess. Adelyn screamed. Both Noah and Ethan looked on in shock.

Gun back on Adelyn, Harlon fished a cell phone out of his back pocket and dialed with one hand. "It's all under control," he said into the phone. "Give Travis his mama and then head on back with everything." He snapped the phone shut, stuffed it back into his pocket, then shoved Adelyn into the corner with Ethan and Noah.

Harlon approached Ron's moaning, fetal body; gun pointed at Adelyn and her boys as he went. With his free hand, Harlon unzipped his fly and started urinating on Ron's head. "You were right, Ron...gonna be one *hell* of a long night."

CHAPTER 8

BONITA SPRINGS
SOUTHWEST FLORIDA

In the same clothes he'd worn on the ride from the airport, Dan Rolston had fallen dead asleep in one of several recliners by the pool. A gorgeous and considerable lanai the size of a small one-story home housed his slumber. It was only dusk, and by napping he was being a rude guest, but the simple fact was that he'd been over-stimulated. Never had he seen such a beautiful home of both extravagant décor and endless luxury. As far as Dan was concerned, he'd have been just fine playing out the remainder of his visits right here under the lanai and all the heavenliness therein: the trickling sounds of its many little waterfalls throughout a massage for the ears; the sunset, the exquisite greenery here and beyond, stone sculptures chosen with an aesthetic hand, the periodic scuttling of pleasant little anole lizards across the mesh walls of the lanai a massage for the eyes.

But now as he stirred, his senses filtering back little by little before the sudden burst of realization that he'd fallen asleep waking him like a good slap, Dan rolled off the recliner and hurried through the rows of sliding glass doors leading into the kitchen. There, Elizabeth and her parents were standing around a marble-topped island, a glass of wine for each of them.

"Well, look who's up and about," Elizabeth said.

Dan rubbed sleep from his eyes. He wished he could rub away the flush of embarrassment he felt burning his face. He did not address Elizabeth, but Russ and Vicky when he said, "I am so sorry for falling asleep."

Russ waved a hand at him. "Please don't apologize. We're happy you could relax."

"Any more relaxed and you'd have to check my pulse," Dan said.

Lame joke, but they laughed.

"Something to drink, Dan?" Vicky asked. "We have wine, beer, scotch..."

A scotch would have hit the spot and been the final seal on his anxiety, but beer seemed the more appropriate answer. Better to not let them think he wanted the hard stuff.

"A beer would be great," he said.

Russ went to the fridge and returned with a bottle of Miller Lite. He handed it to Dan who thanked him.

"I'd have gotten that for you," Russ said, gesturing to the unopened bottle, "but my hands..."

Dan twisted off the cap and said, "Oh, no problem." And then, because Russ had brought it up: "What's wrong with your hands?"

"Arthritis."

"Yikes," seemed like the thing to say. "How long has that been bothering you?"

"Since I retired. You'd think retirement would have eased it some. If anything, it's gotten worse."

Russ had been fortunate to retire at fifty-five. He and Vicky had been forty when Elizabeth came along. Now, with Elizabeth thirty and her parents seventy, she'd expressed to Dan that the age gap, while a non-issue as a child and teen, had been a subject of concern as the years went on and the unavoidable breakdowns of age accrued along the way.

Russ shrugged. "Can't fight father time no matter what you're doing, I guess. Ask Vicky's knee."

"Your knee still bothering you, Mom?" Elizabeth asked.

"Oh yes," she answered with an exasperated face. "It has become my nemesis."

Dan smiled.

"Are you still taking the Celebrex, Dad?"

Vicky answered. "He goes and gets these shots now. What's it called, Russ?"

"Enbrel."

"Is it helping at all?" Dan asked.

Russ nodded. "I think so. I only just started."

"As long as he can still golf," Vicky said with a roll of her eyes.

"Big golfer, Russ?" Dan asked.

"I like to think I'm still his first love," Vicky answered for him again. "Some days I wonder."

Everyone chuckled.

"You play golf, Dan?" Russ asked.

Dan hated golf. Why he'd asked Russ about it with such vigor would be added to the spectacularly enormous *Stupid Shit Boyfriends Say to Suck up to Dad* file. "Does miniature golf count?" he asked with a sheepish smile.

They laughed.

Vicky said, "That's more my speed as well."

"She's now two up on you, Russ," Dan said, daring to dig his way out of the infamous file. "My favorite is becoming less and less of a contest."

More laughter. They sipped their drinks. All was very well.

CHAPTER 9

The Roys initially wanted to do it back at their place. But then transporting live bodies would be more cumbersome. Better to do it here, and transport them after.

Only Adelyn Daigle had been permitted a chair, Ida Roy happily holding a knife to her throat while Harlon and Tucker attended to the Daigle boys. Noah and Ethan were bound at the wrist and ankles, Harlon then shoving them into the corner where they'd fallen hard next to their father.

Their father.

Harlon and Tucker hadn't even bothered with Ron; blood loss was the Daigle patriarch's binds. The logs of meat that had once been his legs lay useless on the floor in a pool of red. His pallor had reached the final color in its palette of sickly whites before death would come and swap it out for degrees of gray.

If the Roys didn't hurry, they would lose him before he could bear witness.

"Mama," Harlon said. "Go on and give Tucker the knife. It's him that needs to be doing this for Jolene and the baby."

Ida Roy handed the knife to her son. "You do it right, Tucker Roy."

Tucker took the knife from his mother, took Ida's place behind Adelyn's chair, and held the knife to her throat.

"*Please…*" Ron moaned from the floor. "*It was an accident…*"

Tucker continued as if Ron had said nothing. He placed the point of the knife below Adelyn's eye. Adelyn whimpered as Tucker tapped the steel tip against her lower lid. "Eye for an eye, ain't that right, Ron?" Tucker said.

"*No...please no...*"

Harlon addressed his brother. "Maybe we should just keep her, Tucker. Left you without a missus to keep you warm at night, didn't they?"

Always the stone face, but the hate in his response seething, Tucker said, "They surely did."

"How is she, Ron?" Harlon asked with a grin. "She know how to please a man?"

Ron writhed and grimaced as though the comment hurt worse than his legs.

"Y'all have no right," Ethan Daigle muttered next to his father.

Harlon's grin dropped. "What's that, boy?"

Louder now: "Y'all have no right. We were never in the wrong. Y'all got no one to blame but yourselves."

"You truly are a mouthy little shit," Ida hissed. "And I *will* do your tongue."

Noah, long since losing the struggle to contain his tears, nudged and urged his brother to keep quiet.

"Well, what do you reckon is fair then, Ethan?" Harlon asked with mock impartiality.

Ethan answered all the same. "You letting us go, of course. Any wrong-doing you think needed fixing has been done with my daddy's legs. You of all people should know the struggle that'll bring a man, Mr. Roy."

Harlon burst out laughing. "The pair on this one! By God if I'm not starting to like the little bastard." Harlon lifted his pant leg and revealed his prosthetic limb, dirty and worn with abuse. He rapped his knuckles on it. "You thinking your daddy's fixing to get a pair of these now, do you?"

Ethan's disturbed expression was his reply.

Harlon smirked. "Tell you what, boy: we *can't* let you go, but because I like you, I'm gonna do you a favor...I'm gonna let you feed your daddy's legs to my babies. How's that sound?"

Ida Roy's sudden laughter was a cackle.

Ethan's bravado visibly sank. Noah's crying became sobbing. Ron moaned and writhed and pleaded.

Tucker waited until they were all watching before he slit Adelyn's throat.

Tucker Roy was washing the blood from his hands in the Daigle's kitchen sink when Ida approached. Both Ethan and Noah could be heard crying in the den.

"What're you scrubbing for? Just gonna get 'em dirty again on them two," she said, motioning towards the den.

"We ain't killing those boys," Tucker said, switching off the faucet and reaching for a dish towel.

"And just why the hell not?"

"Because they're *boys*, Mama." Tucker finished drying his hands, tossed the towel on the counter, and headed back into the den.

Ida followed close behind. "This one here is fifteen!" she said, jabbing a finger towards Ethan. "You was wetting your pecker well before that!"

"We got our eye for an eye and then some. It's done. Can't just go around killing people without cause, Mama," Tucker said.

"*Without cause?*" She jabbed another finger towards the boys. "Them there are witnesses!"

Tucker didn't reply.

Ida spun towards Harlon, threw a thumb back at Tucker. "Your brother's proposing we leave 'em be!"

Harlon shrugged. "His call, Mama. This was about Jolene and the baby."

Ida threw up her hands. "My boys are turning into a couple o' faggots is what it is!"

Harlon laughed.

"I ain't proposing we let 'em *go*, Mama," Tucker said.

"Alright then, just what the hell *are* you proposing?"

"Put 'em to work for now. Make them row us back to our place. Bodies and all."

"And after that? We fixin' to adopt, are we? Two more mouths to feed? Mouths I'd sooner *shit* in than place crumb one?"

Harlon laughed again.

"I don't know, Mama," Tucker said. "We'll think of something. You should know your boy well enough to know he wouldn't do anything to put this family at risk."

Ida looked Tucker up and down, a blatant sneer of judgment on her face. "Thought I did."

Tucker said nothing.

Harlon clapped both hands together once as though breaking a huddle. "Alright, enough of this. You boys ready down there?" He nudged both Ethan and Noah with his foot. "Ethan, I reckon you take your daddy, seeing as how you're the biggest. Noah, you'll be taking your mama." Then, with a little smile: "And don't you boys go using up all your strength with the lifting, you got some rowing to do after."

CHAPTER 10

"We won't be back late," Vicky Burk insisted.

"Mom, it's fine," Elizabeth said.

Dan gestured around the luxurious home. "Yeah—we'll manage somehow."

Vicky smiled and went to give Dan a hug, then stopped mid-action. "You gonna behave this time?"

Dan, who was now pretty sure the Burks were awesome, still burned another red face. All the same, he managed: "It won't be as fun, but okay," and gave her a hearty hug.

"We won't be long," Russ said. "We bought tickets for this thing months ago. Long before we knew you were coming."

"*Dad...*"

Russ nodded and hugged his daughter.

He gave Dan a handshake and a pat on the shoulder. "Glad you're here," he said.

Those words; the way he said them. Dan felt like Russ was Santa telling him he'd been good all year.

Once they'd left, Elizabeth turned to Dan. "Be right back."

Dan shrugged and wandered about the kitchen. He thought about grabbing another beer, stopped, then said screw it and opened the fridge. When he shut the fridge door, Elizabeth was standing there in just a towel. He flinched a little.

"Damn...sneaky girl."

A coquettish smirk. "Mr. Rolston, I understand you're down here researching a book?"

Dan, no fool in the blessed ways of role-playing, responded: "I am, yes."

"How do you research the love scenes?"

"Very thoroughly."

Elizabeth headed out the row of sliding glass doors towards the hot tub. She let her towel drop, and the tub's bluish glow cast a tease of swirling light and shadow over the profile of her naked body. She eased into the bubbling water, turned, and beckoned Dan forward with a single finger.

I love my job, was the last PG thought Dan entertained before joining her.

CHAPTER 11

Whiskey woke Ethan and Noah Daigle.

Harlon Roy, standing over the Daigle boys, both bound and strapped to the same bed, was spitting grinning mouthfuls of warm whiskey into their faces until they woke.

When Ethan had opened his mouth to object, Harlon managed a healthy spit of whiskey into the fifteen year old boy's mouth. Ethan had instantly choked, as did Harlon, on laughter.

One window existed in the room, the shade drawn. Sunlight was rimming the edges of the shade, but it was weak. Ethan guessed it just past dawn. What time had they fallen asleep? Better still, *how* had they fallen asleep? Mama and Daddy had been killed before their very eyes, the boys forced to lift their bodies, row them back here, to the Roy place. The notion of sleep after was ludicrous. And then it became quite clear to Ethan that they hadn't fallen asleep; they'd passed out, their bodies shutting down with enough horror and exertion to fell any man, let alone boys.

Boys.

Ethan was no boy. Tall and strong for fifteen, he was nearly a man, and in the demanding environment in which they lived, some might *say* a man.

But Noah was a boy. At thirteen he'd yet to reach puberty, still held the strength and voice of any girl his size. He'd bested

Travis Roy in their fight because Travis was of similar pre-pubescent stature; no physical advantages lay with either boy. Skill had won the day, to which Ethan, a renowned scrapper growing up in his nook of the Everglades, had been more than generous in sharing with Noah throughout the years.

Except teaching your brother to punch and duck was, well, teachable. How could he teach his little brother to endure something like this? A boy could give up after one too many thumps. The damage on his face could and would heal. What about the mind? How many thumps could the mind take? Ethan was certainly no psychologist, but he was intuitive enough to know that damage to the mind didn't heal as quickly as a good shiner did—especially when the shots being thrown were this debilitating.

"Busy morning, boys, busy morning," Harlon said. "I promised you could help feed your daddy to my babies, didn't I? Make a promise, keep a promise." He grinned. "Two birds, one stone." He then paused in thought, scratching his scraggly chin. "Let's see if I can get one more. Early bird gets the worm? Nah—don't fit. How about, early gator gets the arm? Or leg? Or *head*!?" He burst out laughing and left the room.

Ethan could still hear him laughing outside as he prepared his congregation of gators for breakfast.

CHAPTER 12

"Excited, Dan?" Russ Burk asked.

Dan, in the backseat of the Lexus with Elizabeth as it cruised southeast down U.S. Route 41 towards the Everglades, swallowed a yawn and said, "Very excited."

"Sounds like he's still asleep," Vicky said from the passenger seat.

Dan made an effort at a chuckle, swallowed another yawn and said, "I am the antithesis of your daughter when it comes to mornings."

Elizabeth smiled and rubbed Dan's knee.

"You still an early riser, Liz?" Russ asked.

Dan answered for her with playful disdain. "Oh yes. Six-thirty every morning. No alarm. Not even caffeine once she's vertical. I don't know how she does it. It's like she *wants* to be awake."

Elizabeth cozied up to Dan. "I want to be awake and be with *you*." She burrowed her head into his shoulder like a puppy.

Dan recoiled as if the puppy had never bathed. "Make her stop."

Russ and Vicky smiled.

Elizabeth pulled away. "Fine. Can we get grumpy some more caffeine so he can start resembling the guy I like?"

They'd had coffee at the Burk's before leaving, but the blend was a weak half regular; half decaf. Dan wanted to cry when he saw the container on the counter—the axiom of perceiving something as half-empty never so apt—but didn't think it appropriate to ask and see if they had something with more bite.

So he'd had two big cups black, and hoped for the best. It was not enough, and his yawn machine refused to die. Ask Elizabeth, and she'd say his grumpy machine too.

"Would you like some more coffee, Dan?" Vicky asked.

To sound like a high-maintenance dick or not? "Uh, no that's okay. I'll be fine." A martyr dick. Even worse, genius.

Never one to miss an opportunity, Liz said: "Honey, don't be a sissy. If you want coffee, just say so."

If he didn't know his girlfriend's dry wit better, Dan would've added emasculated dick in there as well. So he forgave her with a little shove, and said: "I suppose this sissy wouldn't mind a little more caffeine."

"I wouldn't mind a Diet Coke," Vicky said to Russ.

"There's a little market about ten miles out from where we're going. We can stop there," Russ said.

"You sure it's not a bother?" Dan said.

"Not at all," Vicky said. Then, turning around to face Dan with spooky eyes and matching voice: "It'll give us all one last look at civilization before we drift off into the unknown…"

Dan returned a grin and said, "Still my favorite. Come on, Russ, you're gonna need to show a little hustle."

"I'm driving *and* paying!"

CHAPTER 13

Harlon pulled the thick rope fixed to the wooden hatch and let the trapdoor slam open onto the deck. He peered down into the large square opening with a proud smile. Below were his babies. All six, often floating to the borders of the sizeable moat encasing them and the Roy home, were now crowded together in one spot, open mouths and endless rows of teeth skyward, waiting.

It was feeding time.

Behind Harlon, a giant white cooler like a refrigerator on its side sat humming. Inside the cooler was breakfast for his babies—chickens, small mammals, chopped deer.

Next to that breakfast, stacked on top of one another, lay the bodies of Ron and Adelyn Daigle—blue-gray skin, rigid throughout, and still intact.

Ida Roy appeared by her son's side as he was reaching for the first chicken.

"So what's the plan then?" she asked.

Harlon dropped the chicken and a tangle of jaws went for it. "What do you mean?" He dropped another chicken. A second tangle of jaws, more competitive than the last.

"You know what I mean. With them in there." She gestured towards their home, where Ethan and Noah remained.

"Tucker and I was discussing it earlier. We ain't decided just yet."

Ida became agitated. "You and Tucker was 'discussing it' were you? And just where the hell was I?"

Harlon dropped a third chicken. "You were still sleeping, Mama. Wasn't about to wake you."

"Well maybe you shoulda, seeing as how your 'discussing it' didn't amount to much."

Harlon cast a funny eye on her. "What's wrong, Mama? You seemed okay enough with things last night..."

"'cause I thought things would be sorted come morning. Now I see the two of you ain't sorted squat. Tucker puttin' ideas in your head?"

Harlon stopped feeding his congregation and faced his mother. "You needn't worry about Tucker, Mama. My baby brother's harder than a stone pecker. You know that."

"I know he's grieving over Jolene and the baby. Maybe he's not thinking right."

"And yet he's over the Daigle place now, cleaning up all traces we ever been. *His* idea to do that."

"Okay fine, good. But then he needs to get rid of *all* traces. That means them boys in there."

"Says it's not necessary."

"Doesn't make any damn sense!" Ida's chest was heaving. "Used to be the two most ruthless boys around. Now you've gone and turned full-faggot on your Mama!"

Harlon laughed. Ida slapped him. Harlon took it without flinching and fought the urge to keep laughing.

"Them boys in there," Ida began, "you think keeping them alive is some kind of charity, do you? They had front row seats to what you boys done to Ron and Adelyn. And then you carrying on about making them feed Ron's legs to your flock."

Harlon fought another urge to laugh. He waved an innocent hand. "Ah, I was just having a little fun, is all. I ain't gonna do it, of course. Besides, I sure recollect you laughing when I said it, Mama."

Ida carried on with her train of thought, refusing to acknowledge her son's fact. She pointed to her own head now. "Killing their *minds* is what you already done, Harlon Roy! Them boys are never gonna be the same no matter what you and Tucker got planned. You'd be doing them a favor by ending it all right now, not to mention wiping up every last bit that might trace things back to us. Sheriff might be afraid to ruffle the feathers of the likes of you and Tucker, but even *he* won't turn a blind eye to no murder when those boys *do* decide to talk one day."

Harlon expelled the last of his need to laugh with a defeated sigh. "Ah hell, I know you're right, Mama. I'll speak to Tucker again when he gets back."

"*We'll* speak to Tucker when he gets back."

Harlon shrugged. "I'm telling ya, Mama, his mind seems pretty made up."

"And so just what the hell is he suggesting we do with these boys then?"

Harlon shrugged again. "Don't know. But you saw him in there with Adelyn—cut her throat and made sure everyone was watching. When he thinks it's in the right, he don't hesitate."

"Well then I guess we need to prove to him that getting rid of those Daigle boys is in the right."

Harlon dropped a hearty leg of deer. "I suppose we do."

"Travis," Ida said.

"Huh?"

"We let him think he's putting Travis in danger by keeping those boys alive. Already lost his wife and unborn, he'd sooner take his own than lose Travis."

"Oh come on, Mama, he's been working like a dog to shield Travis from all of this. Boy's been at a sleepover with lips sealed since."

"And when he comes back?"

"Up to Tucker, I suppose."

"You ain't supposing shit."

"I'm just not letting it bother me now is all. We'll think of something, Mama. Have a little faith in your boys."

Ida sighed, yet her cynicism still blazed. "Fine. But this mess, this is yours and Tucker's responsibility. I ain't involved with caring for those little shits, lessen Tucker wises up and decides to do the right thing. Then I want all parts of being involved."

Harlon smirked. "Apple don't fall far, do it, Mama?"

"I guess we'll see, won't we?" She turned abruptly and went inside.

Harlon chuckled and shook his head. He then looked up as he heard the faint motor of Tucker approaching on the river, could just make out the chainsaw sitting next to him on the boat. Time to get to work.

CHAPTER 14

Russ pulled the Lexus into the gravel lot. There were already a handful of vehicles, most of them weather-beaten pickup trucks that had logged six digits a lifetime ago. The Lexus was assuredly the new rich kid at the school of hard knocks, but money talked at this particular school, the language tourism. And while snide remarks and belches of contempt might well be the norm once he left, to his face, Russ and his brood would be welcomed with open arms.

Next to the lot stood a solitary shop the size of a one-story home. It was white and worn, the cracked and jagged strips of paint revealing the scorched wood beneath adding to its charm, as opposed to making it stand out as the renovation beggar it was.

A short walk beyond the shop, a dock—it too with its cup out for renovation—kept a row of fan boats in line. Beyond that, the whole world was swamp wilderness.

Liz squeezed Dan's arm and snuggled in close, an eager smile on her face as she looked up at him. "Excited?"

Properly caffeinated, Dan's exuberance was an easier sell. "Very." He gripped his notebook in his left hand and glanced at it, a boy about to play with a new toy.

Russ returned from the shop flashing four tickets. "All set."

"We're getting Sam, right?" Vicky asked.

Russ nodded. "Guy at the shop said he was bringing in a crew now, and then he'll be ready to take us out."

Vicky turned to Dan. "We had Sam last time. Wait until you meet him." Vicky puffed herself up and mimicked a big man. "Big, burly guy—as nice as they come. Like a southern Paul Bunyan."

Russ chimed in. "If there's something in the Everglades he doesn't know about, it's not worth knowing." Russ glanced down at Dan's notebook right after, a proud smile on his face.

Dan wanted to hug the guy. Such kindness to a stranger. Sure, he was dating his daughter, but Dan was a stranger to *him*, wasn't he? His daughter could have been dating an asshole this whole time, for all he knew. And yet still, unconditional kindness. Dan felt a contradicting emotion of wanting to both protect and push Russ away; he was too nice a guy for this world...or there had to be something ugly about him, he just hadn't seen it yet.

And the writer's pessimism for the world continues un-abated. Maybe try switching it off for a while, Mr. Half-empty?

"This is just too awesome," Dan said, absorbing Russ' proud smile and lobbing back his own of earnest gratitude. "Really, thank you so much."

Russ waved a hand at him. "Just enjoy yourself, and take lots of notes. I want this to be a bestseller."

"Now *that* would be nice," Dan said.

"Burk?" A heavy voice said behind them. "Burk family?"

Russ raised a hand. "That's us."

Holy crap, it is *a southern Paul Bunyan,* Dan thought as the big man approached. *The boots, the jeans, the red button down with a white long-sleeve tee underneath, the beard. All he needs is an axe and a blue ox. Maybe he has a blue gator somewhere. And doesn't he sweat to death in all that stuff?*

Dan got to ask once Russ and Vicky were finished informing Sam of their trip with him last year, how they'd requested him for doing such a wonderful job, and how they were here for Liz's boyfriend's latest book.

"Don't you sweat to death in all those clothes?" Dan asked, after shaking Sam's hand.

"Ah, it's not so bad. The boots and sleeves keep the creepy crawlies out—" He brought up both hands and wiggled his thick fingers to mime said crawlies. "Plus, I'm sure they'll tell you, it can get *pret*-ty breezy once I gun us through a couple of channels."

"That it does," Vicky said, holding up a windbreaker.

Sam pointed at Vicky. "Now there's a swamp vet."

Vicky took a bow.

Sam laughed and then clapped his big hands together in one loud pop. "Okay! Shall we get a move on?"

CHAPTER 15

Sam was seated up high in the driver's seat towards the back of the boat, controls in both hands like giant joysticks, the massive fan behind him like the back of an emperor's throne. Russ and Vicky were seated at the bow, Dan and Liz behind them, closest to Sam. Dan had asked for this seat so he could pick Sam's brain when the fan wasn't blasting.

It wasn't now, and Dan started picking away. "So the whole python problem *is* overblown?" he asked.

Sam nodded, steering them into a quiet inlet. "They're out there, but not in the crazy numbers the media would have you think. That python hunt last year you were talking about? Something like 1,600 hunters volunteered. Guess how many they got?"

Dan said, "Less than a hundred."

Sam pointed at Dan with a little smile. "He *does* do his homework."

"But weren't many quick to say that they netted so few because the 'hunters' were merely volunteers with no experience in catching pythons?" Dan asked.

Sam nodded. "Definitely some truth to that. In fact, they've gone and cancelled this year's hunt. Decided instead to focus efforts on *training* folks to look for pythons properly. Better than a bunch of 'hunters' out there blasting away at anything that twitches in the bushes." He winked at the Burks and they laughed. "Still, they're out there—some of 'em big suckers—but they typically don't bother us. Not unless they're provoked. And even then, they usually won't make us a meal."

Dan eagerly nodded along; it was all stuff he'd researched before, but so very cool to hear it straight from the mouth of a hardened local like Sam. "We're too big, right?" Dan asked.

Sam nodded. "Well, *we* are. Don't know about those two—" He gestured to Vicky and Liz with a little smile.

"Oh stop it, you" Vicky said with a little shiver.

"Seriously though," Dan said. "I've read reports about snakes and children. Surely they can't differentiate between a child and a small adult?"

Sam raised an eyebrow at Dan, and then gauged Vicky and Liz's reaction.

"*Dan,*" Liz said.

Dan splayed his hands. "What? It's a legit question." He turned back to Sam: "I think it would make for a great scene in my book if someone was swallowed by a snake. Obviously, I don't want to make it a kid, so maybe a small adult would be believable?"

Sam gave Vicky and Liz another uncertain look.

Vicky waved a hand at him. "It's fine."

Sam shrugged. "Sure—I guess it's believable; they swallow gators and deer. Still unlikely though. Can't see a python having many opportunities for something that doesn't live in the wild. And that's the real problem with these snakes. Raccoon numbers alone have dropped more than ninety-nine percent in the last decade."

"*Ninety-nine percent?*" Russ said with disbelief.

Sam nodded, a saddened look on his face. "Opossum and bobcat aren't far behind with those numbers."

"Bobcat?" Liz said. "They can catch a bobcat?"

"Well, not so much *catch* as *surprise*. Pythons are like gators in that they tend to lurk and wait, grabbing you when you're not ready. Masters of peekaboo."

"Yikes," Russ murmured.

Dan jotted down Sam's words, then turned to Liz. "I didn't know the small mammal population had been affected *that* much. That might come in handy."

Liz rubbed his knee. "Glad it helped. Though I think my mother now has a date with a snake nightmare later tonight."

Vicky grunted in agreement.

Dan leaned forward and touched Vicky's shoulder. "I appreciate the sacrifice, Vicky."

"I expect to be on the acknowledgment page."

"Deal."

Sam smiled at their banter, and then began maneuvering the boat slowly into a narrow channel. Mangrove trees lined both sides of the channel, their spindly gray roots above water and tangled together into yards of thick fencing.

"Ready with that windbreaker, Mrs. Burk?" Sam asked.

"Yes, sir." Vicky put the windbreaker on.

Now to the group: "You folks ready to fly?"

All eager nods.

Sam gunned the engine, the giant fan behind them roared, everyone whooped with excitement, and Dan would have sworn they actually did fly the entire length of the channel.

CHAPTER 16

Travis Roy came home to find no one there.

"Daddy? Meemaw?"

"Travis?"

It was coming from Uncle Harlon's bedroom. Only it didn't sound like Uncle Harlon.

He asked anyway. "Uncle Harlon?"

A loud whisper now. "*Travis.*"

Travis inched towards his uncle's door, placed his ear to the wood. "Who's there?"

"*Travis, open up!*"

Was that Ethan Daigle?

Travis opened the door. It *was* Ethan Daigle. And Noah Daigle. Tied up together in his uncle's bed.

"Travis, you gotta cut us loose!" Ethan said in an urgent whisper.

Travis squinted as though trying to work out a riddle. "What're you all doing in my Uncle Harlon's bed? Why're you all tied up?"

Ethan sat up as far as his binds would allow. "Travis, listen to me: your daddy and uncle killed our folks. Now they're fixin' to kill *us* next. You gotta cut us free."

Travis frowned. "Daddy and Uncle Harlon did what?"

Ethan gritted his teeth, his loud whisper growing louder. "*Killed* our daddy and mama, and then tied us up in here. Only a matter of time before they get 'round to killing Noah and me next. You gotta cut us loose, alright? Travis?"

Travis took a step back and automatically touched the gator tooth around his neck. "I don't believe it."

Ethan's frustration flushed his face. "Believe your own eyes, don't you? How do you explain us being tied up like this?" Ethan gave a futile tug on his binds. "And we *seen* what they did to our folks! Made us *watch*!"

Travis shook his head adamantly, tears now rimming his eyes, his angst not because he didn't believe, but that he was desperate *not* to believe. Because if true, it was his fault. All of it. He knew how his daddy and Uncle Harlon could be when it came to family. And hadn't he known there would be retaliation for what happened to Mama? Yes. But not like this. Never could he have imagined something this bad. Chief among these sobering truths—and it had always *been* chief; just quiet since his mother's accident, Travis' simple-mindedness gifting him with an effortless ability to suppress, to subconsciously bury all that was scary as easily as pulling the covers up over one's head to make the monsters go away—was that the accident with Mama would have never happened in the first place if it hadn't been for his lies.

But now that simple-mindedness would *not* suppress. It was not a deep dig, after all. Did not require extensive tools of manipulation. Though no physical evidence of Mr. and Mrs. Daigle's demise was shown, a bound Ethan and Noah, coupled with their words, was enough to bring everything to the surface intact.

His fault.

All of it.

Travis started full-on crying now.

"Travis!" Ethan said. "Travis, stop! *Travis!*"

Noah spoke. "Travis, I forgive you."

Travis stopped crying and looked at Noah. He wiped tears from his eyes and sniffed hard. "Huh?"

"I forgive you for lying," Noah said. "About the fight. About Ethan joining in. I forgive you. You *won't* burn come judgment...not if you do the right thing now and cut us loose."

Ethan's anger became an instant eagerness. He followed his younger brother's lead and spoke with the urgent whisper again. "That's right, Travis. You cut us loose now, and you can make it right. All will be forgiven."

Travis stepped towards the bed. And Ethan and Noah recoiled in fear. Travis frowned, confused. Then he felt and saw his meemaw's twisted hand on his shoulder.

Ida Roy chose to stay in Harlon's room with the Daigle boys while she lectured her grandson. She wanted them to hear.

"What was done was what needed to be done. You was there, Travis; you saw what happened to your mama."

Travis, his gaze never leaving his meemaw's—not from want, but because she kept a firm grip on his face with both hands, keeping their eyes locked on one another—said, in a timid voice: "But Mr. Daigle too?"

Ida cocked her head, studying the boy, scanning him for any rare signs of reason or empathy that needed snuffing. "Mr. Daigle too. An example needed to be made, boy. You take from a Roy, and we take it right back, and then some."

"What about them?" Travis asked, eyes gesturing to the bed behind him because his head could not.

"It's your daddy's call. He reckons letting 'em go is the right move."

Ida watched Ethan and Noah's reaction out of the corner of her eye, saw the faintest glimmer of hope, and it fueled her performance that much more. "Problem is, Travis, I worry about what might happen to *you* if your daddy did such a thing."

"Me?"

Ida nodded. "We let these boys go and they're going straight to the police. And them police will see fit to locking up your daddy and Uncle Harlon for what they done. Already lost your mama; you wanna lose your daddy too?"

Travis shook his head in his grandmother's hands.

"You will if we let these boys go." Ida took a hand off Travis' face and pointed to her head. "Your daddy's not thinking right. He's too upset about what happened to your mama and their unborn. He needs you now, boy. Your daddy needs you. You got to convince him that getting rid of these boys is the right thing to do, lessen you want to see your daddy fry for what he done; Uncle Harlon too."

Travis shook his head again. He looked hypnotized by Ida's words.

"A liar!" Ethan blurted from the bed. "Your Travis is a liar! All of this is his doing from the start! He just gone and *admitted* to us before you come!"

Ida, her hands still on Travis' face, looked over her grandson's shoulder with an expression of neither malice nor worry, but total calm, as if the game's outcome was all but sealed. "I was at the door the whole time, boy. I heard nothing of the sort."

"*What!?*"

"Oh, I heard you offering forgiveness for this *lying* you keep going on about, but I never heard a confession from Travis' mouth—only you offering forgiveness."

"So why was he carrying on with tears and that!?" Ethan asked. "An innocent boy wouldn't let guilt stir him up so!"

"Clever boys like you gettin' into his head is what done it." She took her gaze off the Daigle boys and looked into Travis' eyes with her one and only expression of warmth. "Our Travis has always been more heart than know." She ran a gentle finger over his cheek.

"Fine!" Ethan said. "Let's ask him now then. Travis, tell her. Tell her it was a fair fight between you and Noah. Tell your meemaw this whole thing was your doing from the start. Tell her!"

Ida kept hold of her grandson's face, kept the one look of warmth on him full blast. "Travis?" she said.

"All will be forgiven, Travis!" Ethan said. Travis chanced a glance over at Ethan. Ethan flicked his chin skyward. "*ALL* will be forgiven!"

"Travis?" Ida said. "It's pretty simple, isn't it? Get rid of these boys and keep your daddy. Or let them go and be a pitiful orphan who knows in his heart he as good as killed his own flesh and blood."

Travis nodded and walked out of the room without looking back.

Ida turned and gave Ethan and Noah a wicked little grin, intentionally baring her rotted teeth. "Job done," she said.

CHAPTER 17

The fan boat glided down another channel, far wider than many of the previous they'd ventured. "Going deep, deep into the swamp now, folks," Sam said.

They passed a small cabin to the right of the river. An old man walked out his front door and onto the wooden deck supporting his rustic little one story home. He waved and smiled at the boat. Sam waved back, the rest of the group right after.

"He live there?" Dan asked.

"Yes, sir."

"Geez…" Vicky muttered, turned in her seat and still staring at the old man smiling from his front porch as they glided past. "Imagine that?"

Sam smiled. "Most folks who live this deep don't know any other way of life. Don't crave any other way either. They like the solitude."

"And what do they do when an alligator walks into their living room?" Vicky asked.

"Turn them into boots?" Dan said.

"That old guy didn't look like he was killing any alligators to me," Liz said.

"Oh, I beg to differ," Sam said. "You don't make it to being an old man out here without knowing how to deal with the wildlife. That old fella would give a nosy alligator one *hell* of a surprise if it tried to wander into his living room."

Everyone but Sam joined Vicky in glancing back at the old man on his front porch, their previous looks of uncertainty now ones of quiet awe.

They continued down the channel, Sam periodically pointing out wildlife that some had missed, Vicky and Russ snapping photos, Dan scribbling in his notebook now and then, usually after asking Sam a question.

It was Vicky who first spotted the tree blocking their way.

Frowning into her viewfinder, she lowered her camera and turned. "Sam? I see something up ahead."

Sam sat up and squinted down the river. "Tree down?" he muttered, more to himself than his passengers.

"That's what it looked like to me," Vicky said.

Sam continued the boat forward. Soon, everyone could see it—an enormous cypress tree on its side, smack dab in the middle of the river. No boat was getting by.

"This isn't right," Sam said, again more to himself than the others. He killed the engine and guided the boat towards the base of the tree, bumping it lightly with the bow as they floated to a stop.

"Was there a storm last night?" Russ asked.

Sam responded as he maneuvered towards the bow to inspect the cypress' trunk. "No, no storm." Then, with a paradoxical look of both discovery and mystery, he added: "Besides, no storm's doing that—" He pointed to the very base of the cypress trunk.

Everyone looked, the boat rocking under the sudden shift of people.

"Looks cut," Liz said.

"It *was* cut," Sam replied.

"Does this happen often?" Vicky asked. "People cutting down trees and just leaving them in the river?"

"No," Sam said, still inspecting the trunk. "At least I've never come across it. People 'round here would show a bit more respect for the environment."

"So then what do you think happened?" Liz asked.

Vicky answered: "Maybe someone did it on purpose?"

"Why?"

"To block our way?"

Liz turned to Sam. "What do you think, Sam?"

"I don't know," he replied, leaving the bow and heading back towards the stern. "Your mother's guess sounds as good as any, I suppose."

"Why would someone do that?" Dan asked.

"No idea," Sam said over his shoulder as he bent to retrieve something at the base of his seat. He eventually stood upright, holding a grappling hook. The iron claw was four-pronged and enormous, the size of Sam's head. It was fastened tight to a long coil of thick rope that Sam was now uncoiling from one hand to the other.

"What's that?" Vicky asked, wide eyes stuck on the thick iron prongs of the hook.

Sam gave her a reassuring smile. "Call it a big fishing hook… particularly helpful in removing downed trees from the water."

"Are you going to remove it then?" Liz asked.

"Gonna try." Sam bent again and came back up with a large crossbow.

"And what's *that*?" Vicky said.

Again, Sam gave a reassuring smile as he brandished the crossbow. "This here fires the big fishing hook."

"Wait," Dan said.

Sam glanced over at Dan. "What's up?"

Dan didn't quite know how to phrase it. "Well…don't you wanna know *why* the tree was there?"

"I already know why," Sam said. "To block our way, keep me from doing my job."

Dan felt a twinge of frustration at Sam's refusal for foresight. "But somebody put it there for a *reason*, didn't they?"

"Yes," Sam said, the tiniest bit of condescension creeping into his tone, "to block our way. I've been up and down this river a million times, Dan. Nothing up ahead I haven't seen; nothing we need to worry about." Sam started loading the grappling hook onto the crossbow. "Besides, I'll be doing the Roys a favor. And that's never a bad thing."

"Who are the Roys?" Dan asked.

"Family who lives further down the river. Got a bit of a reputation for being...not nice."

"Would they have done this?" Russ asked. "To keep people away maybe?"

"Nah. One of them—Harlon—farms gators for nearby parks and what. He's got his own little farm right there on their property. Sometimes he'll let me bring up a group to get a look during feeding. Can't imagine he'd want to keep people away of such a thing. Be bad for business."

"I thought you said they weren't nice," Dan said.

Sam sighed and shrugged. "Well, to put it simple; they're not. But there's business, and then there's...everything else I guess. The Roys can smile with the best of them if it'll bring them money. But behind those smiles...well, it's kinda like the gators they own. In the right conditions, you can get close to them, pet them, get your picture taken, but you can't ever forget who you're dealing with. That make sense?"

"Like a waiter who smiles no matter how much you complain, then goes in back and spits in your food," Liz said.

Sam chuckled. "Sounds about right. Only replace 'spits in your food' with 'plucks out your eye' and then maybe you're on to something."

"Uh..." Dan began, "well, then at the risk of stating the obvious; why would we want to go near these kind of people?"

"The Roys might be a bit ornery, but they're not stupid. If they ever did anything to me or my group—or any *other* driver and his group—they'd be in deep water. Forgive the pun."

"We didn't see them last year, did we, Sam?" Russ asked.

Sam shook his head. "No—you'd remember if you'd done so. Harlon's gator farm—heck, *Harlon*—is something you wouldn't soon forget."

A moment of quiet unease came over the boat. Sam set the hook and crossbow down and addressed the group. "Aw, now listen, folks; we don't have to do anything you don't want. You don't want to see the Roys' gator farm, consider it crossed off the schedule. I just figured Dan would want the best tour possible for his book, is all."

Dan felt ashamed at all the hesitancy he'd been voicing, the picture it might paint to Liz and her parents. That picture being one of a big ol' pussy. Not the image he wanted to portray to a girl who might very well be his wife one day, and especially to the man and woman who might be handing Liz over to him if that special day should come. He envisioned Russ shaking his hand and leaning into his ear: *Take care of her, son. Try not to be a pussy.*

"I say we do it," Dan all but blurted.

"You sure?" Liz asked.

"Hell yeah, I'm sure. Sam's right—we want the best tour there is, right?"

Liz turned to her parents. "You cool with that, Mom and Dad?"

Vicky said, "Fine with me."

Russ agreed.

"Alright then," Sam said with a smile, bringing his big hands together with his trademark clap that sounded like a gunshot. He then bent and picked up the crossbow.

Now loaded with the iron claw, Dan thought the device looked like a potent bit of weaponry straight out of the middle ages. Still, he played the role of eager helper, the far more familiar portrayal of hesitant skeptic buried under a mountain of ego. "So what do we do first, Sam?"

Sam brandished the crossbow again. "Firing it is the fun part. Dragging the tree to shore once it's hooked? Not as fun."

"Let me guess," Dan said, "you're firing; I'm dragging."

Sam laughed. "I see why you're a writer—got the plot figured out already." He squeezed Dan's shoulder. "Believe me, brother; if they'd let me, I'd let you fire this baby until your fingers bled. And don't you worry, we'll *both* be pulling." He glanced back at Russ and Vicky with a playful grin. "Maybe *all* of us."

Vicky donned an overly pretentious face and blew on her fingernails in true diva fashion. "I just had my nails done, I'm afraid."

"Me too," Russ said.

CHAPTER 18

The sound of a chainsaw was audible to all as the boat drifted to a stop at the base of the Roys' bridge.

"*Hello!?*" Sam yelled.

The consistent roar of the chainsaw was unyielding.

Sam did a quick job tying off the boat to the small wooden ladder leading up to the bridge; he had little worry of drifting in the river's shallows, but felt it might give his group peace of mind to see the act. He now turned to them. "They won't be able to hear us over that racket. I'm gonna head on up and let them know we're here. No swimming while I'm gone," he said with a wink. He headed up the small ladder, and then started across the bridge towards the Roy home.

Sam crossed the bridge and then followed the sound of the chainsaw. The roar of the saw was strongest around back. He followed it, expecting to see Harlon or Tucker Roy hard at work on an addition to their deck, hoping they would spot him first, hoping he wouldn't have to tap the shoulder of a man with a chainsaw—a *Roy* with a chainsaw.

Sam saw only Harlon. Harlon did not see him. And Sam had never been so grateful in his life. Because Harlon was sawing off the leg of a dead man.

Sam instantly turned and started back towards the boat.

The sound of the chainsaw stopped behind him. Silence was never so loud.

Sam kept on, praying the saw stopping was Harlon finishing whatever in God's name he was doing, and not spotting him as he turned and fled.

"That you, Sam?" A voice behind him. Harlon's.

Bluff. You didn't see anything. Not a damn thing. Bluff until you can get to the boat. Bluff.

Sam turned. Harlon was there, wearing a yellow blacksmith's apron, not caring that it was spattered with blood.

"Hey there, Harlon," he said with a smile that felt frighteningly transparent. As for his tone? He was surprised his greeting didn't come squeaking out. Sam was a big man. A tough man. But what he'd just seen? Nothing in his lifetime could have prepared him for that.

Harlon took a step forward.

Don't back up. If you back up, he'll know.

"What, you got a group with ya?" Harlon asked.

Sam nodded. "That's right. Thought I'd bring them by to see your farm—" *Sell it, sell it, please God help me sell it.* "But I couldn't find you. Was about to give up and call it a day."

Harlon nodded slowly, but said nothing. He then looked down at his apron, at the slick spatters of blood everywhere. "Was sawing up some lunch for my babies." He wiped off some of the blood. "Make a mess, don't they?"

Sam smiled. It felt a little better this time. Now another bluff. A *huge* bluff. But could he sell it? "Sure looks like it. What was it? Deer?"

It sounded good. Natural. Only a fool would have attempted such a bluff. And Sam felt therein lied the beauty of it: Harlon knew him; knew Sam *was* no fool.

Harlon nodded. "That's right—deer. Big one too."

The relief Sam felt just then was orgasmic. "Well, then I guess I'll let you get back to it. Good seeing you again, Harlon."

Sam turned towards the bridge.

"Where're you going?" Harlon asked.

Sam turned back. "I got a group waiting. Remember?"

"Thought they wanted to see my farm."

Sam held up a hand. "Ah, it's okay, Harlon—you're busy. Some other time."

"They comin' back?"

Sam frowned, confused. "Coming back?"

Harlon took another step forward. Again, Sam fought every urge to back up.

"You said *some other time*," Harlon said.

"Yeah, sure—I'll bring another group some other time."

Harlon took another step forward. They were within handshake distance now.

"What about this group?" Harlon said. "*This* group won't get to see."

Sam wanted to run for it. It was possible. Everyone knew Harlon Roy had a prosthetic leg. But the time it would take to untie the boat and cast off? Time enough for Harlon to grab a gun. Time enough for him to get a bead on all of them.

"Oh well—" Sam gave a lame little chuckle. "That's the way it goes, I guess."

Harlon looked disappointed. "I guess."

"Well, I better get a move on. Got another group to take out after this. Maybe I can swing them on by?" The bluff to end all bluffs. And damn clever too, if he did say so himself. Mentioning a group waiting for him after this one; he would be reported missing sooner than later if something were to happen. Risky prospects, even for a crazy like Harlon Roy.

Harlon seemed to consider it, looking away for a moment, scratching his stubbly chin. When his eyes settled, he turned his gaze back on Sam and smiled. "I look forward to it, Sam."

He extended a bloodied hand.

That's human blood.

And then a second internal voice, more adept at self-preservation: *Just shake it. Shake it and go for Christ's sake.*

Sam shook it. And Harlon used his left hand to jam a knife deep into Sam's eye, hitting the brain and killing him instantly.

Sam dropped at Harlon's feet. Harlon wiped the blade and then tucked it away in the same apron pocket from where he'd snatched it. Without pause, he then bent and grabbed Sam by the ankles and began dragging him back towards the rear of the house. "Sorry, Sam," he said as he dragged. "I always liked you. Wrong place at the wrong time, as they say."

Harlon left Sam next to the remains of Ron and Adelyn Daigle, removed his apron, and went inside. After a brief word with only Ida (Tucker gone fishing with Travis), Harlon grabbed his pistol, tucked it down the back of his pants, and headed towards the bridge to introduce himself to Sam's group.

CHAPTER 19

Tucker Roy cast his line, sat back in the boat, and cracked a beer. The talk with his son about their current predicament was necessary, but he wasn't looking forward to it.

"Travis—" he began, but got no further.

"Daddy, I don't wanna be an orphan."

CHAPTER 20

"Here comes someone," Liz said.

"That's not Sam," Vicky said.

The approaching man crossed the bridge towards the boat. He was tall and wiry and walked with a limp. He was smiling the whole way.

Stopping at the end of the bridge, he looked down into the boat and, still smiling, said: "You must be Sam's group."

"That's right," Russ said. He pointed to his own chest. "Russ Burk." Then gestures all around: "This is my wife Vicky; my daughter Elizabeth; and her boyfriend Dan. And you are?"

"Harlon Roy. Sam told me to come on down and collect you."

"Where is he?" Vicky asked.

"Sam?" Harlon Roy pointed up towards the house. "Told me he wanted to give you folks a treat, so I let him get things started." He smiled again.

Liz spotted a spatter of blood on Harlon's gray tee. Harlon's eyes followed Liz's gaze until his chin was on his chest, studying the spatter. He gave the stain a casual wipe as if shooing away a bug. "Occupational hazard, ma'am," he said. "Not too many vegetarian gators."

Liz gave an uneasy smile.

"So, you folks ready to see my babies?"

Dan, seeing an opportunity to assert himself, said, "Actually, if it's all the same to you, we'd rather wait for Sam. If you tell him we all said that, I'm sure he'd understand."

Harlon's smile dropped a little. "But only *you* said that," he said to Dan. "You want me to lie, do you?"

"No, no—I just meant if you told Sam we'd prefer if *he* came down here to get us…"

Harlon only stared back.

Dan gave a nervous clear of his throat. "Is something wrong?"

Harlon shrugged. "Just waiting for you to finish your sentence. Not much of a mind-reader, boy."

Dan waved both hands with an olive branch smile. "Haha, okay. All I meant was that we've been with Sam all morning, and—" *What? Don't trust a guy with blood on his shirt, who Sam told us was both mean and a little nutty? Yeah. Hell yeah. But how to say such a thing to said mean nut in a bloody shirt?* "I'm just thinking we might all feel more comfortable if Sam came down here to bring us on up, that's all. We didn't mean any offense." He looked at Russ, Vicky, and Liz, hoping for nods and murmurs of agreement. He got them, and felt relief—sort of.

Harlon Roy sucked air between his teeth with a brief flash of disgust. "Didn't mean any offense, huh?"

Dan shook his head quickly. "No, not at all."

Harlon called over his shoulder while keeping his eyes locked on Dan. "Sam? Sam, you come down here a minute?"

No answer.

"*Sammy?*" Harlon called again.

Nothing but the ambient sounds of the river around them.

Harlon brought his stare back on Dan. "Doesn't surprise me he can't hear. He's 'round back, fixin' to get a hearty meal prepared for my babies—for what was *gonna* be your show."

Russ finally spoke. "You know, I think we got off on the wrong foot, Mr. Roy. We're very grateful; talk to Sam and he'll tell you. In no way whatsoever did we mean any disrespect, and if we offended you, please accept our apology now, sir."

Harlon smiled at Russ almost instantly. "Apology—and a *damned* good one—accepted, Mr. Russ Burk. Calling me *sir*, even." He looked at Dan. "Could take a lesson or two from your old man, boy."

Dan was about to correct Harlon on the status between he and Russ, but correcting Harlon after the damage control Russ had just managed seemed anything but wise. He merely nodded and smiled at Harlon instead. Neither Liz, nor Vicky, nor Russ sought fit to make the correction either. In any other situation, the misunderstanding might have been cause for a brief moment of bashful smiles all around. Now it seemed as if everyone was on Dan's page—a correction, no matter how minor, seemed akin to flicking the tiger's nose once it'd finally dozed.

"So," Harlon said, eyes on Russ, and only Russ, something Dan felt was deliberate, a metaphorical castration for all to see. "Am I taking you nice folks up to see my babies get their lunch, or am I sending Sam back down to call it off?"

The boat exchanged looks. Russ, his ego perhaps fed just enough to cloud judgment for calming the waters with a man who was the total antithesis of his country club chums, said: "Let's head on up and watch your babies get their lunch, Mr. Roy."

Harlon did not lead them to the rear of the house. He led them to the far right, towards the hatch that opened into his gators below. Grabbing the thick rope in the center of the hatch, Harlon grunted as he pulled the trapdoor open and let it slam back onto the deck as he always did, a Pavlovian sound to his congregation: come and get it.

Liz and Dan peered in first, saw the spiraling impatience of dark green bodies, their powerful tails slapping the water and each other, their mouths open wider than logic would suggest, the seemingly limitless rows of razor teeth stretching logic further still.

Liz jumped back at first sight.

Harlon laughed.

"Wow, they're aggressive," Dan said.

"Been around a lot of gator farms during feeding, have you, boy?" Harlon asked Dan.

Dan stood upright and looked at Harlon. "No, I haven't."

"Then what the fuck would you know about it?"

Russ and Vicky had just started to peek down into the hatch when they heard Harlon's comment to Dan. They stopped. All four faced Harlon now.

"Where's Sam, Harlon?" Russ said.

"What happened to 'sir'?"

Russ took a deep breath and let it out slow. It was an exhale of fear, not frustration. "Sir, where's Sam?"

"Why'd you folks move that tree? Didn't you think it was there for a reason?"

Vicky inched close to Russ' side, Liz to Dan's.

"I said that to Sam," Dan said. "Those exact words, actually. He insisted we move it."

Harlon shook his head, looking almost disappointed. "Big dummy should have just let it be...I liked Sam, dammit."

Vicky was now tight to Russ' arm as though trying to stay warm. Dan began inching Liz behind him.

Harlon dropped his head and began muttering like a man bitching about his job. "Damn tree was there for a reason... should have just let it be...fucking Daigle boys to worry about—" Then, with a jolt, Harlon's head shot up to full attention, eyes wild and angry. *And now I got YOU FOUR to consider! God DAMN if this isn't a big old fucking mess!*

"SAM!?" Russ suddenly yelled.

Harlon blinked at Russ, all traces of anger suddenly gone.

"SAM!?" Dan joined in.

Now Harlon looked at Dan, his expression equally quizzical. Calmly, he asked: "What are you people doing?"

"Where is he?" Russ asked. "Where's Sam?"

Harlon's chin recoiled in disbelief. "He's *dead*, dummy. What'd you think I was going on about?"

Dan immediately spun and urged Liz, Russ, and Vicky towards the bridge. "Go, go, get to the boat and—"

Harlon rolled his eyes, pulled his gun, and shot Dan in the back of the head. Blood hit Liz's face. Dan crumbled to the deck, dead eyes open, one of them blinking involuntarily. His left leg twitched.

Vicky dropped her camera and screamed, turned and burrowed into Russ' chest like a child desperate to avert its eyes. Russ held her tight, his face a mask of fear.

Liz stood frozen in shock, the blood of her dead boyfriend dripping down her face.

"I'll say the same thing to you folks as I said to Sam," Harlon said. "It's nothing personal; just the wrong place at the wrong time." He glanced down at Dan's body. "Though I gotta say, I didn't care much for this one—got a smart mouth on him." Harlon rolled Dan over to the open gator hatch with his foot, and then kicked him in.

When he heard the thrashing below, and then the unmistakable sounds of eating, Russ let go of Vicky and vomited.

CHAPTER 21

Tucker Roy rowed his son home. The talk did not go as he'd expected.

Tucker had no intentions of lying to his son. He'd planned to tell him that he *did* kill Adelyn Daigle, that Harlon *did* kill Ron Daigle. Their family had been horribly disrespected, and two of their own—Travis' mama and his unborn brother or sister— had been taken from them. Something so terrible demanded retribution. They'd been in the right.

But Tucker hadn't been able to get to any of that. Instead, Travis had blurted something about orphans, going on about his fear of losing both his mama *and* his daddy.

Tucker had been initially stumped on why the boy was conjuring such ideas, yet he'd soon settled on part of the grieving process. And why not? Lost your mama; worried about losing your daddy next. Made perfect sense. And then there were the Daigle boys. They were orphans now. Not some meaningless word to be slung with spite in the schoolyard, but the real thing— there, tied up in their home, both parents gone forever.

So when the subject drifted into the territory of the as-yet-unknown future of the Daigle boys, Tucker believed he'd understood what his son had been alluding to all along—he didn't want to be as good as an orphan, with a mama in the ground and a daddy in prison. And it was now Tucker's job to convince his son that no such thing would happen.

When Travis softly said that the only way for no such thing to happen was to kill Ethan and Noah Daigle, Tucker stopped rowing.

And so now, as Tucker Roy rowed his son and himself closer to home, he reflected on their talk, his son's final pleas:

> *"So you won't let them take you away, Daddy?"*
> *"No, son. Nobody's taking me away."*
> *"You're not going to jail?"*
> *"I'm not going to jail."*
> *"You promise?"*
> *"I promise."*

His promise—what Tucker knew had to be done with the Daigle boys in order to keep it solemn—was spoken with sad conviction, but conviction nonetheless. He recalled his daddy's words to *him* as a boy, right after his daddy testified against an innocent man in order to cover up a crime his uncle had committed:

> *"There are things in life you just gotta do, boy. Don't mean you gotta like 'em. This was family."*

Tucker nodded at the memory, his conviction feeling sturdier. He forced himself to recall similar memories, where difficult decisions were made according to the Roy script, except Travis suddenly broke his daze.

"Someone at the house, Daddy."

Tucker looked ahead. A fan boat was tied to their bridge. It was empty. He frowned. "What the hell?"

CHAPTER 22

Tucker and Travis inspected the fan boat tied to the short ladder of their bridge.

"Whose is it, Daddy?"

Inspecting as he spoke, Tucker said: "Commercial boat. Tours."

"They come to get a look at Harlon's flock, maybe?"

Tucker instantly stopped inspecting and looked at his son. His stone face twitched at the possibility. "I suppose that could be right." Tucker had told Travis about Ron and Adelyn Daigle; what had to be done. What he hadn't told his son was that Tucker and Harlon thought it best to dismember the couple and feed them to Harlon's congregation, something Harlon had promised to do while he and Travis were fishing.

Suppose someone happened along while Harlon was…busy?

The screen door up ahead banged. Ida Roy appeared and hurried across the bridge to meet them. She didn't look herself. Tucker couldn't tell if it was anxiety or aggravation. His mother was not the easiest read.

"Mama?" Tucker called up to her as she approached.

Ida stopped by the ladder. She looked down at her son with folded arms. "Come to your senses then?" she asked.

Tucker ignored the question. He gestured at the fan boat. "Mama, what is this?"

Now it was Ida who ignored the question. "*You come to your senses?*"

Tucker left the boat alone for a moment and gave Ida his full attention. "I suppose I have." He turned to Travis. "Stay here, son." He climbed the ladder and stood close enough to his mother so that Travis couldn't hear. "I woulda come around on my own, Mama. Didn't need you using Travis like that."

Ida poked her son in the chest. "You needed to be coming around sooner than later, boy. Couldn't afford to wait for people to start sniffing around until you figured what was right."

Tucker looked away and gave a little nod. "Fair enough." He looked back at his mother. "When it comes to this family, I'll cut the throat of any man or woman. But them boys in there…" He gestured towards the house and then looked away again. "I suppose I was just hoping there was another way is all."

"*Ain't* no other way," Ida said.

Tucker brought his eyes back on his mother, a shimmer of irritation in them. "Told you I come around, Mama. No need to keep going on."

"Daddy?"

Tucker turned and glanced down at his son. Travis was standing on shore by the fan boat's side, running a curious hand over it. "Did Meemaw tell you why it was here?"

Tucker turned back to Ida. "Well?"

Once again it seemed as if Ida chose to ignore the question. "So you come around on what needs to be done with them Daigle boys, huh?"

Tucker sighed. "Yes, Mama."

"Cut any man or woman's throat for this family?"

"On Daddy's name."

"Good." Ida glanced down at Travis. "You stay put, Travis, you hear?"

Travis nodded.

Ida brought her gaze back on Tucker. "Follow me."

Harlon and Ida brought Tucker into Harlon's room. When Tucker saw that Ethan and Noah had three new roommates, Ida turned to her son and said: "You come around on the Daigle boys, then you should have no problem with these three."

CHAPTER 23

Harlon took a swig of whiskey from the bottle and handed it to Tucker. Tucker didn't acknowledge the bottle.

"Oh, what was I supposed to do, Tucker? Sam *seen* me cutting up Ron Daigle! I'm supposed to just let him get back in his boat with his group so they can hurry on back and report us?"

Tucker looked out onto the river. "Goddamn if this ain't the biggest fucking mess."

"Said the exact same thing, little brother." He handed the bottle to Tucker. This time Tucker took it.

"And there was a fourth one?" Tucker asked after taking a long pull from the bottle. "Another man?"

Harlon nodded. "Trying to play hero is what he was doing. Forced my hand."

"He 'round back with Adelyn and Ron?"

Harlon smirked and looked away.

"I miss the joke?" Tucker said.

Ida tapped her foot on the deck a few times.

Tucker looked at his mother's foot, frowned for a second, and then got it. "Cut him up and fed him to your congregation already? Told me you hadn't even tossed in Ron and Adelyn yet."

Harlon reached for the bottle. "I haven't."

Tucker pulled the bottle away. "You *haven't*? Explain that."

Harlon reached for the bottle again, his gesture implying: no whiskey, no explanation.

Tucker handed it to him.

"Boy went swimming in one piece," Harlon said.

"Thought you said it'd be best if they were in pieces? Drop them in whole and it might take days. *Your* words."

Harlon swigged the whiskey, some of it dribbling onto his chin. "Was an accident, little brother. Had to shoot him by the open hatch. Fell right in after. I'm supposed to go in after him?"

"And if they don't finish their supper, your congregation? If this man's remains find their way into the river?"

Harlon frowned. "And just how the hell would that happen? My babies ain't getting out, no way a dead man is."

"Their phones? IDs? Personal belongings?"

"Taken care of. Got two nice cameras out of it all."

"Best get rid of them."

"Or sell 'em. Keep us in good whiskey for a spell." Harlon grinned.

"Or get rid of them," Tucker said again, no trace of compromise on his stone face.

"'bout as much fun as a case o' crabs, you are."

Tucker thought for a moment. "And if more folks come by? Folks like Sam, wanting to see your flock?"

Harlon laughed. "How bout I just say *no*, little brother?"

"Alright then," Tucker said. "Suppose someone comes by, not wanting to see your flock, but fixin' to find out what happened to Sam's group?"

Ida stepped in. "*Then they'll be fixin' to find out what happened to Sam's group.* Got nothing to do with us. If anything, they'll be pointing fingers Sam's way. People start to notice those folks are missing, and the first place they'll check is Sam's rental spot. That's assuming them folks told anyone where they were going this morning. That could be days from now."

Tucker reached for the bottle again. Harlon handed it to him. Tucker took three deep swigs, shaking his head on the last one as though shaking off a good punch. "They'll come looking for Sam first," he eventually said. "The boat especially. His rental probably cares more about that boat than Sam."

Ida stepped forward and took the bottle from Tucker. She emptied the remains over the railing and into the river. Harlon objected, but Ida shot him a look that silenced him like a bullet.

"You'll be good for shit if you're both piss drunk before right gets put right," she said.

Harlon chuckled.

"And how are we putting it right?" Tucker asked.

"Well, first thing you'll be doing is dealing with Sam's boat," Ida said. "You leave it tied up by our bridge and it won't take no genius to figure out we're involved."

Tucker looked at Harlon. "What do you reckon?"

Harlon shrugged. "Shouldn't be too much of an issue. We can pull it to shore 'round back, cover it good. Be invisible from the river."

"Gotta get rid of it eventually," Tucker said.

"*Eventually*," Ida said. "Right now, it needs moving."

"And when that's done?" Tucker asked.

Ida gave her son a cautious look. "Come 'round on killing them Daigle boys; you telling me you've got pause on them three *strangers* in there?"

Tucker said nothing.

"Cut a man or woman's throat for this family, ain't that right, Tucker Roy?" Ida said.

"I know what I said, Mama."

"And yet you stand there looking like a little boy, unsure which hole to put his pecker in."

Harlon laughed.

"Mama, you can stop. I'm gonna do what's right," Tucker said.

Ida moved close to her son, looked up at him with an icy stare. "And what do you reckon 'right' is, boy?"

"I reckon 'right' is we remove all traces to save this family."

Ida, dark gaze unyielding behind her thick lenses, said: "And how do you reckon we remove all traces?"

The stone face Tucker wore for every occasion was fixed tight and equally unyielding as he stared down at his mother. "We kill 'em all and feed them to Harlon's flock."

"'bout fucking time your balls was in plain sight." She turned to Harlon and then back at Tucker, addressing them both. "It's past three. Get to taking care of that fan boat while you still got the light."

CHAPTER 24

Ethan and Noah Daigle had been in the same room, the same bed, and the same binds ever since they'd first entered the Roy home. They'd been given water but no food. When they'd needed to urinate, Harlon told them to piss the bed—and they did. When they'd needed to defecate, Harlon told them they could shit the bed if they wanted, but didn't recommend it on account of the smell they'd be locked in with. Both boys held it.

Now, the room ripe with the smell of urine and sweat and fear, Ethan and Noah had new roommates. Two women and a man, all three bound by the wrists and ankles as they'd been, save for being tied to the headboard of the bed.

The new occupants had entered the room in three very different states.

The man, small and lean and what Ethan guessed at roughly seventy, was pleading continuously, begging Harlon and Ida to let them go as mother and son set about tying them up. He'd offered money, promises to keep quiet, anything. Harlon and Ida just continued without acknowledgment as if the man were babbling a foreign language.

The older of the two women, petite and an equally fit-looking seventy, the man's wife no doubt, cried non-stop—sobs when the binds were cinched tight, sniffles when there was a brief lull, and back to sobs when the binding would resume again with merciless force.

And then there was the younger of the two women. Ethan guessed her maybe twice his fifteen years, if not younger. No guessing was needed to see that the woman was a spitfire, constantly shouting obscenities at Harlon and Ida. When Harlon paused for a moment to declare that he should have *"kicked this bitch down the hatch with her fucking boyfriend,"* Ethan came to the frightening conclusion that there had been a fourth. More frightening still, was the way Harlon had confessed to dispatching that fourth. Ethan knew all too well what lay beneath that hatch.

And so now, after an hour together in the room, after the man had plead himself hoarse (he had not stopped when Harlon and Ida had left the room, merely continued pleading towards the locked door with futile hope); after the older of the two women had cried herself dry; and after the younger of the two women had used up every obscenity she knew (she too had not stopped after Ida and Harlon had locked them in, often bickering with her father as he'd told her to stop so that they might listen to his reasoning, she telling him he was wasting his time, they were screwed); all three were spent. And it was time for introductions, to share how they'd all managed to find themselves in this communal hell, and most importantly to Ethan, how they were going to escape.

CHAPTER 25

The fan boat was moved around back as planned.

"Look at this here," Harlon said, still on board. He hoisted the crossbow in one arm, the big grappling hook in the other. "Guess this explains how they moved the tree."

"Leave it be," Tucker said. "We got to cover it yet."

"*Leave it be?* These here beauties are now *mine*, little brother." Harlon grinned like a kid with new toys as his head volleyed between crossbow and hook.

"Fine, take 'em," Tucker said. "Can we get to covering now?"

"Patience of a bullet," Harlon muttered, tossing the crossbow and grappling hook onto the bridge. "Here, what's this?" He bent and came up with a notebook, started leafing through it.

"What's it say?" Tucker asked.

"Hard to tell. A lot of chicken scratch." Harlon flipped to the front page. "*Dan Rolston*—that's the name on front. I'll betcha that's the guy I booted down my hatch in one piece. I reckon the nerdy little fella was keeping a journal of his trip."

"'Booted' into your hatch, huh?" Tucker said. "Told me you had to shoot him and he *fell* in."

Harlon glanced up from the notebook. "What, you keeping a journal too? It happened like I said."

Tucker just shook his head. "Let's get to covering."

Several green and beige tarps were soon draped over the full length of the boat, cloaking it to even the keenest eye. It became, as Harlon had predicted, invisible from the river.

"I reckon we take care of Sam first while we still got the light," Harlon said as they waded their way around front, knee-high boots sloshing in the dark water. "Can't see Mama approving of us running that saw indoors." He chuckled. "Once Sam's cut up, and we drop him down the hatch along with Ron and Adelyn, we can go inside and deal with the others. Don't need daylight for that. We can snuff 'em tonight and get to cutting first thing in the morning."

Tucker grunted and continued wading ahead of his brother.

Harlon flashed a cagey eye at Tucker's back. "Meant what you said, did you?"

They reached the short ladder leading up to their bridge. "'bout what?" Tucker said.

"Killing them folks along with the Daigle boys and feeding them to my flock."

Tucker stopped as he was preparing to climb the ladder. He looked back at Harlon. "Of course I did. You ever know me to lie?"

Harlon grinned. "Sure have."

Tucker frowned. "Lie to *family*?"

Still grinning, Harlon said, "I can recall a whopper or two you told Jolene when you and I come stumbling in at dawn."

Tucker's frown darkened. "You don't get to talk about Jolene just yet."

Harlon looked away and nodded. "Okay, little brother. Still, I gotta wonder if it don't warrant asking—from me, not Mama."

Tucker now turned completely and faced Harlon. "Well, go on and ask then. And get it over with sooner than later. I'm getting tired of answering the same questions from my own damn kin."

"Just seems you turned a quick corner on the whole ordeal is all."

"Seems I had nowhere left to turn."

Harlon chuckled. "Always did have a clever way of putting things, little brother." His smile dropped suddenly, Harlon's typically carefree face the rare spectacle of grave. "We don't have a choice, you know. We didn't go looking for none of this. Hell, you think I wanted to give up my room?"

Tucker nodded slowly, his gaze on the river, mind somewhere else. Finally, he said: "Should have thought it through better with them Daigle boys."

Harlon gave a quizzical tilt of the head. "Just made a fuss about all that—tired of being asked by kin, you said."

"That's not what I meant. I meant involving them from the start. Making them watch me kill their mama, you their daddy. We could have never let them go after such a thing—don't know how we thought otherwise."

Harlon's eyebrow went up. "Don't know how *you* thought otherwise."

"Say again?"

"Maybe we didn't talk it through well enough at the time, but I'd be lying if I didn't think we were all on the same page."

"So you were fixin' to kill those boys after?"

Harlon shrugged. "I suppose I was."

Tucker looked out onto the river again.

"Oh, come on, little brother—just what the hell were you planning to do with those boys if you weren't fixin' to kill 'em?"

Gaze still on the river, Tucker said, "I don't know. I was so crazed about what happened to Jolene and the baby, I couldn't think about anything but inflicting pain on that family. I wanted Ron and Adelyn to die, I know that, but I never really considered those boys."

Harlon gave a humorless snort. "And yet you made 'em watch when you cut their mama's throat."

"I did make 'em watch, yes...I felt like they needed to be punished for what'd been done. I guess it's the after I never gave much thought to...or was *able* to give thought to."

Harlon splayed his hands. "And so now what? They been punished enough in your eyes? That it?"

"Maybe it is."

"Maybe it *was*, not *is*. Said you come around."

Tucker took his eyes off the river and placed them on his brother. "I *have*."

Harlon sighed. "Don't think of it as murder, little brother. Hell, us Roys, we might be some crazy motherfuckers, but we're no *murderers*. We didn't seek these folks out like a bunch of psychos. All of this—*all of it*—is other folks' doing. We did what needed to be done, and we were in the right. Now we just gotta clean it up, is all."

"Don't mean we got to enjoy it," Tucker said.

Harlon gave his brother a curious look. "Enjoy it?"

"Haven't seen concern one on your face since this all began. Hell, I should drop dead in the water if you aren't having a little fun."

"You know me, little brother—I can find a good time in the most peculiar of places."

Tucker shook his head. "It's like Daddy said—some things you gotta do; don't mean you gotta like 'em."

"Maybe you don't remember Daddy the way I do."

"Said it though, didn't he? Said it to me the day I asked him about lying to get Uncle Jake free; send that other man to jail."

Harlon nodded. "He said it…but don't you go fooling yourself into thinking Daddy was all broken up about it. Uncle Jake and him were on the town later that night, celebrating the result until the whiskey and their peckers were sucked dry."

Tucker glared at his brother. "The pair on you, suggesting Daddy sought the bed of another."

Harlon burst out laughing. "Just where *did* you come from, little brother? Never did understand why you was so faithful to Jolene. Not like she would have dared leave if you wanted to wet your pecker in some other piece of ass, ya pussy-whipped little—"

Tucker blasted Harlon with a hard right hand, launching his brother backwards into the river with a hefty splash. Harlon surfaced with a gasp, wiping water and blood from his face.

Tucker pointed a threatening finger at his downed brother. "You can call me pussy-whipped until you're hoarse for all I care. But you refer to my Jolene as a 'piece of ass' again, Harlon Roy, and I *will* make sure you don't come up for air next time."

Harlon smiled. "You feel better now, do you, little brother?"

"Fuck you."

Still smiling, Harlon got to his feet and began massaging his jaw. "I remember you packing more of a punch. Maybe Mama's right—maybe you have gone faggot."

Tucker started up the ladder. "Keep talking, you one-legged gator-fucker."

Harlon burst out laughing again.

CHAPTER 26

"*Escape?*" Liz whispered. "And how are you planning on doing that?"

"Noah and I are fixed to this damn headboard. Try as we might, we're not going anywhere. But you folks aren't fixed to anything. You could get to your feet if you wormed around enough."

"And then what?" Russ said. He gestured over his shoulder, to his wrists bound together behind his back. He then pecked his chin at both his wife and daughter, bound in identical fashion. "Our hands are useless tied up as they are—" He then gestured down towards his feet; they were cinched tight together at the ankles, no slack for even the tiniest of shuffling. "Our feet too. You don't think they'd hear us hopping around in here like giant rabbits if we managed to stand?"

"Harlon and Tucker are outside. Hear that chainsaw buzzing? That's them. As long as it keeps on buzzing, they're as good as deaf."

Softly, her first words since being in the room, Vicky asked: "What are they doing with a chainsaw?"

Liz and Ethan exchanged a glance.

"It doesn't matter, Mom," Liz said. "It's like Ethan said; as long as it keeps making noise, it could help us."

"What about the old lady and the kid?" Russ asked. "They're right out there, aren't they?" He motioned towards the door with his chin. The sounds of television and the smell of cigarette smoke beneath the door were constant.

"She's got that TV turned up pretty good," Liz said.

Ethan smiled at Liz, grateful for her comradery during a moment when it was all easy to succumb to hopelessness.

Russ remained a trickier ally. "Okay then—we get to our feet; they can't hear us hopping around; then what? Our hands are still useless behind our backs. Mine especially."

"Why yours especially?" Ethan asked.

"Arthritis," Liz said.

"I'm all thumbs when it flairs up," Russ said. "And tied up like we are, believe me, it's flaring."

Ethan heard nothing after "thumbs." He was thinking of his friend, Casper Cole.

Casper Cole, who was caught stealing a case of beer from the back of their local distributor when he was fourteen.

Casper Cole, who was promptly handcuffed and tossed in the sheriff's cruiser while the sheriff went inside to talk to the shop owner.

Casper Cole, who was not afraid of what the sheriff might do—a "boys will be boys" slap on the wrist was most likely—but terrified of the hiding he'd get from his drunken old man when the sheriff took him home.

Casper Cole, who then desperately managed to *break his own thumb*, slide his damaged hand out of one of the cuffs, and then crawl out the open cruiser window on that muggy summer night to leg it anywhere but home to his daddy.

"I have an idea," Ethan said. "I'm not sure you folks are gonna like it though."

Ethan told them about Casper Cole. A silence followed. Not one of comprehension, but of cold realization. Ethan was serious in his proposal. And that proposal held far better prospects than the absolute nothing they'd produced thus far.

Question was: whose thumb?

Russ immediately volunteered. Liz immediately opposed him, claiming it should be her.

"I am *not* breaking my daughter's thumb," Russ said.

"What, we should do *yours*?" Liz said. "You just said your arthritis is flaring up, and that you're all thumbs when it does. We break one of those thumbs and what're you left to work with? Do the math, Dad."

"I *am* doing the math. We need you and those two boys as fit as possible to lead us out of here. With my hands and your mom's knee? We're going to be anchors either way."

"And I can throw that argument right back. Youth will allow us to push on despite. It should be one of us three."

"Uh…" Ethan said. "This is gonna sound bad, it being my idea and all—" He jerked at the straps that kept he and Noah's wrists fastened to the board above their heads. "But unless one of you wants to climb up onto this bed and back your butt into me or Noah's face so you can get to our thumbs, it might have to come down to *you* three, though I'm assuming Mrs. Burk is out."

"*Yes*," Russ said instantly.

Ethan nodded. "One of you two then."

"*Dad…*" Liz said, her tone giving every implication that the matter was no longer up for discussion; *she* was the parent on this one.

But Russ needn't even speak to reclaim his status. He looked hard at his daughter; a stern, immovable face Liz remembered when Russ would drop the hammer during her ever joyous teen years of know-it-all-dom. And Liz felt her mind—already defeated by her father's gaze—drifting. What she wouldn't give now to be back in those moments, being reprimanded by her father…safe at home. And although they'd have been strangers at the time, Dan would still be alive, waiting to meet her a decade later.

Oh God, Dan.

Not just gone but…what happened to him after…

A sudden thought hit her without warning, striking like a sucker punch to her core, and she marveled at the morbid complexities of the human mind, its subconscious taste for the macabre. That thought was: *Is Dan* truly *gone?* As in: *Did the alligators finish eating him?*

Liz dropped her head and shuddered.

"Elizabeth?" Russ said.

Liz slowly lifted her head. Her father's stern face was still there, more so. She gave a defeated nod. "Okay, Dad."

Russ exhaled slowly, a strange sense of relief washing over his face despite the truth that he was about to have his arthritic thumb snapped. Perhaps it was the relief only a father could ever know.

"Okay…" Russ said with another sigh. "Okay."

Vicky finally spoke. "Suppose this works, and we do manage to get free. How would we get back without a boat?"

"We could do it on foot," Ethan said. "Work our way through the swamp."

"*On foot?*" Liz said.

Ethan nodded. "Both Noah and I know the way."

"That's not exactly what I meant," Liz said. "Wouldn't we be vulnerable to wildlife?"

Ethan shrugged as much as he could with his hands above his head. "You ask me, the wildlife here—in this house—is far more lethal than anything we're gonna find out there."

There was a moment of pause as everyone digested the comment. The chainsaw continued its merciless buzzing outside, sometimes idling, sometimes revving high right before meeting a resistance that would briefly dull the roar and allow the horrifying reality that it was cutting into something. Something not a tree.

"Alright, let's do this," Russ said. "Ethan? We're all ears."

Ethan looked hesitant.

"Ethan, son, it won't be long before that sawing out there stops—" Russ then flicked his chin towards the door. "Or the old lady decides to check in on us. Let's go."

"My friend Casper was cuffed in front on account of the sheriff not seeing him a threat; just trying to give him a scare..."

"*Ethan*," Russ said impatiently.

"My point is that Casper could *see* what he was doing. He was able to pop it close to the wrist by *lookin' at it*. Tied up the way you are, hands behind your backs, you're gonna be doing it blind." He looked at Liz. "Grab the *whole* thumb—as far down as you can. When you're ready, give it one good jerk down and towards the rest of his fingers. Bend it back the other way and you just broke his thumb in half. Got it?"

Liz nodded.

Russ, not one for cursing, said: "Can we just fucking do it already?"

Father and daughter now lay back to back. Getting into that position—endlessly worming around on a wooden floor with both wrists and ankles tightly bound—was far more cumbersome than Liz imagined it might be. Cumbersome and painful. If her shoulders and hips and neck and every other damn thing had complained during the process, how had her poor father felt? Oh, and just you wait until we get to your thumb, Dad.

Liz gripped her father's whole hand first. He gripped hers back. They could not see one another, but sight would have added nothing to the power of their embrace.

"I love you, Dad."

"I love you too, sweetheart."

Their hands loosened their grip on one another, and Liz grabbed her father's thumb whole.

"Down and towards the rest of the fingers," Ethan said, both he and Noah straining intently to watch from the bed.

"I know," Liz said.

"It's gonna hurt, Mr. Burk—but you can't scream."

"I know," Russ said.

"Liz, make sure you—"

"Ethan, will you *please* shut up?" she said.

"Sorry."

Russ began to wince, preparing for the pain.

Vicky looked away.

"Do it," Russ said.

Liz jerked her father's thumb down and towards his fingers. There was a muffled pop. Russ' entire face became an excruciating grimace, his jaw muscles clenched so tightly that they jutted from the hinges like knuckles. His face was instantly red, nearly purple, like a man struggling to breathe—and he was, for the rapid fire snorts from his nostrils were his only source of exhale, fear that he might cry out if he were to unclench his jaw keeping it nailed shut.

Liz immediately began worming and flopping towards her father so she could face him. She'd witnessed her father wince at the pain his arthritis had caused from menial tasks about their home in the past. She could not even begin to fathom the pain he was feeling now.

She faced him. His face was already wet with the sweat of agony. Russ looked his daughter in the eyes, his face no less red, no less twitchy and desperate to contain a scream, and he actually smiled. And it was a real smile. One obviously tainted by pain, but it was no grimace or placating gesture to assuage his daughter's concern. It was a loving smile, a smile that said he would do it all again for her, that no sacrifice would ever be too great. Liz started to cry.

"Sweetheart," Russ said, finally daring to open his mouth. "Sweetheart, you need to stop. When we get home—and we *will* get home—you and I can sit and cry for days. Right now we need to keep it together, okay? We need to keep it together. You broke my thumb very well; Daddy's proud of you."

Liz gave a half-cry, half-chuckle. She then nodded and wiped her tears on her shoulder. "I'm okay...can you do it? Can you pull your hand free?"

Russ glanced up at the bed. "This isn't going to tickle either, is it?" he said.

Ethan and Noah didn't respond. Their faces, wrought with sympathy, spoke to him instead: *No it isn't, Mr. Burk.*

Russ did not hesitate. He pulled at his binds, his face turning back into that same grimacing picture of agony. His jaw clenched tight once again, his breathing like machine-gun fire through his nose.

For a moment, her father's struggle seemed too intense, and Liz wanted to insist he stop, that there might be another way. But such thinking was akin to changing your mind after you'd already leapt from the plane. All she could do was float next to her father and assure him that his chute would pop open at any—

POP!

Russ' arm flew out from behind his back as though jerked free from some unseen string above. An instant relief washed over his face, and he immediately began moving his arm in circles in an effort to regain circulation.

Everyone but Vicky exhaled simultaneously. Her head had remained turned for the duration, unable to watch her husband's suffering. When she heard the collective sighs—Russ' chief among them—she turned and let out her own, an expression of both love and admiration for her husband's heroics housing that sigh.

With his good hand, the now-loose rope still wrapped around his wrist, Russ used the edge of the bed to pull himself to his feet. He immediately looked down at the binds that held his ankles, bent and started fiddling with them. He soon rose, a frustrated look on his face.

"We need something that can cut. I can't untie them, especially one-handed."

"Start with that dresser over there," Ethan said. "From what I gather, this is Harlon's room—he don't have at least one knife in here then I'm a monkey's uncle."

Russ hopped as delicately as he could towards the dresser.

The TV in the den was still on, the saw outside was still buzzing.

Two more hops.

He lost his balance on the second, colliding with the wall, inadvertently using his bad hand to brace the collision, bringing out an involuntary cry of pain.

All heads whipped towards the door, not the least being Russ'. He was upright now, hand over his mouth, but the damage had been done.

The room fearfully listened for two sounds: the din of the TV dropping, or the thumping of angry feet towards the bedroom door. The latter of which could be negated if the former was not done—sound cloaking sound. It added a cruel jack-in-the-box element of surprise to a moment that was already unsurpassed in its excruciating wait.

They waited and listened.

No TV dropping, no thudding footsteps. This could be good or bad. Sound cloaking sound. They could only wait and see if the jack popped from its box, barging into the room, finding what they'd done.

So now they waited and watched, the metaphorical handle on the box turning slowly, each nuanced pitch from the television a musical ding after a crank on the handle.

One minute. Two.

It was safe now. It had to be. These were not subtle people, Liz thought. If the crazy old lady had heard them—or, somehow, the crazy men with the chainsaw—then the room would have been stormed immediately.

"I think we're good," Liz whispered from the floor.

Russ acknowledged his daughter with a quick nod. He had one hop left to arrive at the dresser. He made it with little to no sound. He began checking the drawers, each one pulled, searched, and then pushed back with antique care.

It was on the third dresser drawer that he spotted the knife. And what a knife. Mr. Dundee should be so lucky.

Russ spun towards the group, brandishing his find. He immediately bent and cut his own ankles free. He went to Vicky first.

"No—" she said, gesturing towards the bed. "The boys first. Once they're free you can hand the knife over to them. It'll be faster."

Russ hesitated.

"Russ, pragmatism trumps chivalry on this one," she said.

Russ hurried towards the bed.

CHAPTER 27

Harlon and Tucker Roy were nearly finished with Sam. His arms and legs were now stacked next to Ron and Adelyn's like fleshy logs. The head and torso remained.

Tucker handed the idling chainsaw to Harlon. "Here—you do the rest."

Harlon took the saw with a smirk. "Gettin' squeamish?"

Tucker wiped a spray of blood from his cheek with the back of his hand. "Tired of gettin' messy. You can have a turn."

"And yet I did Ron Daigle all by my lonesome when you wasn't here."

"And then made me do Adelyn and now Sam. You can have a turn."

"You sure?" Harlon asked. "Head's the best part."

Tucker shook his head and removed his apron. "Nah... you're not having any fun," he said disapprovingly.

Harlon grinned and revved the saw. Above the roar, he shouted: "Told you, little brother—I can have a good time anywhere."

Tucker was still shaking his head as he started towards the house...where the Daigle boys and the Burks had just cut the last of their binds.

CHAPTER 28

The pros and cons of two escape options were quickly discussed.

"I say the window," Russ whispered urgently. "It's nearly dark now. If we're quiet, we'll be home before they even realize we're gone."

"Too slow," Ethan said. "We'd need to go one at a time. I say the door. Only Travis and his meemaw out there. I could put each of them out with one good whack."

"And suppose Harlon and Tucker are there as well?" Russ asked.

"I still hear the chainsaw, don't you?"

Nobody spoke for a tick. The saw was roaring outside.

"It's too risky," Russ said. "Suppose you don't knock them out right away? Suppose they start screaming and hollering just when that chainsaw happens to stop?"

Ethan raised the knife. "Then I'll cut their damn throats—" Tears of rage and sorrow filmed his eyes. "Hell, I plan on coming back and doing it anyway."

"I'm sorry for your loss, Ethan," Russ began. "I can't even begin to imagine what you and your brother must be feeling right now. But please don't let anger cloud your common sense."

Ethan wiped away his tears with a quick, angry swipe of his hand. "I'm just thinking of the fastest way is all."

"Maybe fastest isn't smartest."

In an impatient whisper, Liz said: "Both will be irrelevant if they come in here while we're debating—let's pick one and *go*."

Russ and Ethan exchanged stares, each one vibrating with adrenaline. If they didn't move now, they were inviting death.

Ethan finally sighed. "The window," he said.

Russ patted him on the shoulder, and they all hurried towards the window.

Tucker Roy opened the door.

CHAPTER 29

Tucker Roy had walked through his front door spotted in blood and looking for whiskey. His mother, hypnotized by the television, paid him no mind. His son Travis was as equally uninterested in his arrival; he was stuck to the sofa, his face in one of those handheld video game machines Tucker loathed so much.

Tucker had begun going through the cabinets. He saw a jar of Harlon's moonshine, considered it, and then reconsidered. Harlon's moonshine, despite his insistence otherwise, was 180 proof piss. Tucker wanted real whiskey. Good whiskey.

He'd called to his mother in her chair, asking where it was, but her response was to turn the volume up on the TV. He'd then thought of Harlon again—how he was known to keep the good stuff in his room. Except his room was "occupied" right now. But what did that matter? He didn't have to talk or even look at any of them. He could just enter, go through Harlon's dresser, find the whiskey, and then be on his way.

And so Tucker headed towards Harlon's room and opened the door…

CHAPTER 30

For a brief moment, it was like the scene of an attempted burglary. Intruders by an open window. Intruders freezing instantaneously upon discovery. Homeowner equally frozen as he processed the scene.

Except these were no intruders. They wanted out. And the homeowner, done processing the scene, wanted them in.

Tucker lunged for them, grabbing the first neck he could. It was Liz's, and she cried out. Russ immediately swung his good fist at Tucker's face. The punch landed, yet Tucker hardly noticed as he throttled Liz, both hands around her neck as if he meant to crush instead of choke. Liz gurgled, kicking and clawing up at Tucker futilely. Russ punched again and again, each blow ineffectual; they were the first punches Russ Burk had ever thrown in his adult life.

Ethan shoved Russ aside and rammed Harlon's knife deep into Tucker's gut.

That shot was effective.

Tucker let go of Liz. She dropped to the floor, coughing wildly. Tucker stumbled backwards, grabbing his stomach and wincing as though horribly sick. He hit the wall and slid down, his expression of extreme intestinal distress never changing.

"*Stab him again!*" Noah cried. "*Stab him again!*"

Ethan lunged down at Tucker with the knife. Tucker caught Ethan at the wrist. A brief test of strength ensued, Ethan's hand vibrating with effort as he struggled to push the knife into Tucker's throat, Tucker resisting, pushing back, winning, eventually wrenching Ethan's wrist with one violent jerk, the blade coming free, skidding across the wooden floor.

Ethan, his right wrist stuck in Tucker's powerful grip, resorted to swinging wildly with his left, repeatedly punching down at Tucker's face for all he was worth, the slumped Tucker and his debilitating wound making an otherwise mismatch level.

Noah joined in, kicking Tucker from the side as though he meant to punt his head from his shoulders. Tucker defended himself against both boys as best he could, his grip on Ethan's wrist wavering, the repeated punches and kicks from the Daigle boys beginning to have an effect.

A primal screech pierced the chaos, and Noah spun to see Ida Roy lunging forward, hands outstretched in savage claws, looking to gouge whatever she could latch on to.

"*DIRTY FUCKERS!!!*"

Ida grabbed Noah's face, tearing and raking with ferocious intent. Noah screamed, turned away and began flailing blindly and defensively, desperate to peel the wild animal from his face.

Liz lunged forward, snatching Ida by her scraggly hair, ripping her off of Noah and dragging her towards the dresser where she smashed her head against the wood repeatedly, Vicky joining her daughter, grabbing Ida's hair and adding force to each thudding smash.

Ida would not give, her screeching actually gathering strength with each whack she received. In desperation, Vicky resorted to grabbing and biting Ida's arm. This brought forth another screech that was growing a more potent deterrent by the second; they were angering the beast not destroying it.

Ethan stepped forward, grabbed hold of Ida's hair, and jerked her backwards, the force such that Liz and Vicky lost their own grip. With her scalp in his left hand, Ethan rammed countess uppercuts into Ida's face, the first punch knocking her cold, though Ethan held on, keeping her slack body upright, continuing to punch, the effects of adrenaline blinding him to her unconsciousness...or not.

Ethan eventually let go, and Ida hit the floor face-first. Tucker moaned for his mother, and Ethan spun and slammed a kick into Tucker's face, dazing him, his head and torso lolling to one side. Ethan kicked again and again, Tucker too weak now to defend. Russ pulled Ethan off, Ethan then turning on Russ with wild eyes, demanding a reason why he should stop—and Russ had a damn good one:

"Where's the kid!?" Russ asked. "Where's Travis!?"

Everyone stopped, the only sounds the TV and the constant buzzing of the chainsaw outside. Ethan sprinted for the door and looked out into the living room. Travis was not there.

The buzz of the chainsaw outside stopped.

CHAPTER 31

Ida Roy lie face down on the floor, unconscious. Tucker Roy was slumped over onto his side, semi-conscious and mumbling, his stomach awash with blood.

Travis was gone.

The sound of the chainsaw outside had stopped.

The math was frighteningly clear: Travis had run to his Uncle Harlon plus Travis had told his Uncle Harlon what had happened equaled Uncle Harlon was now headed their way.

"We can't just stand here and wait," Russ said.

"We go to the front door," Ethan said. "We ambush him when he comes inside."

All eyes fell on the open bedroom door, and beyond that, the front door to the Roy home.

"No," Russ said. "He has a gun. We need to run."

"We run and he'll give chase," Ethan said, "shootin' as he does. He'll catch one of us." Ethan glanced at Vicky. "Your wife has a bad knee. What do you reckon the odds are he tags the slowest one? Better we catch him by surprise while we can!"

"He's right," Vicky said.

Russ gaped at his wife. "*What?*"

"I can't run. If we have a chance to end this now, we should take it. I say we jump the son of a bitch the moment he walks through that door."

"Damn right," Ethan said. "Let's move now. He comes through that door while we're in here and we lose the element of surprise."

Harlon Roy appeared at the bedroom window. His eyes were wild and lustful for atrocity.

And no one saw him...their collective gaze was on the bedroom door, considering Ethan's plan.

Liz eventually turned. Harlon was gone. The sound of the chainsaw in the distance came a short moment after.

"Is that...?" Liz asked.

Russ nodded at his daughter. "Sure sounds like it."

"Maybe Travis didn't run to Harlon," Vicky said. "Maybe he just ran. Maybe Harlon doesn't know."

"Well, then I say we just go," Russ said.

Even Ethan nodded at the idea.

"You sure you can lead us out on foot?" Russ asked.

"Blindfolded," Ethan said.

"We just might be," Russ said as he glanced back at the window. It was officially night.

The sound of the chainsaw continued its metallic whine, now sounding as if it was shifting locations, getting closer towards the front of the house.

"Is he out front?" Vicky asked.

"Why would he be?" Russ said.

"Well, it sure as hell sounds that way!"

The sound of the saw seemed to hover out front, periodically idling, and then periodically roaring to life before settling into another droning idle.

"What the hell is he *doing*?" Vicky asked.

Ethan shook his head. "Don't know. Maybe he's...maybe..."

"*What?*"

Ethan dropped his head and spoke softly, as though he'd just been scolded. "Well, the hatch to his gator farm is round the side of the house, closer to the front really. Maybe now that it's dark, he figures it's safer to bring some of his...some of his 'work' that way."

Vicky instantly looked as if she regretted asking.

Ethan gave a small, apologetic shrug.

The saw was on the move again, sounding as if it was heading back the way it'd came.

"He's coming back," Noah said. "He's coming 'round back again."

"Then we need to move now," Ethan said. He began huddling everyone together, nudging them out of the room and towards the front door.

Ida and Tucker never stirred.

They were all at the front door, the sound of the saw distant now. It was time.

"Everyone ready?" Ethan asked.

They all nodded.

Ethan gripped the doorknob. "Once I open this door, we all head for that bridge. Move like your butt's on fire. Noah? Liz? You take lead. Mrs. Burk? Your husband and I will mind you, keep you moving on account of your knee. Once we hit the shoreline, we take hands, and none of us lets go for nothing, you hear?"

They all nodded again, the contrasting emotions of dread and anticipation on each face, the Daigle boys no exception.

"*Now*," Ethan said, and ripped open the door.

Liz and Noah sprinted first, as instructed, Ethan and Russ helping Vicky close behind. The chainsaw continued to buzz in the distance as they all eventually hit the bridge as one, their feet pounding the wood as they hurried forward, desperate to reach the wilderness unseen.

A loud, splintering crack like a tree falling froze them. The bridge beneath them jumped, dropping a few inches. They clutched each other's limbs as they would railings. One final crack and the bridge gave way, all of them plummeting into the river below.

Everyone surfaced with a collective gasp, their faces wide-eyed and stunned, looking freshly slapped.

The sound of the chainsaw grew as Harlon Roy came into view, holding the saw, standing where his bridge no longer began. He killed the motor and looked down on them, floodlights illuminating eyes of a delighted lunatic.

"Looks like you folks had a little mishap," he said. "Reckon it's termites?"

Every face stared up at him, no less stunned and gaping than before.

Harlon set the chainsaw aside and pulled a pistol from behind his back. "If y'all had just stayed put, I'd have made it quick—" He grinned and began scratching his head with the barrel of the gun. "Now I'm gonna have me some fun." He pointed the pistol down at the group and started firing.

CHAPTER 32

Everyone reacted differently to the gunfire. Ethan and Noah dropped, sinking into the dark, shallow water in an effort to eliminate themselves as targets. Russ dove at Vicky to shield her, tackling her in the process, both of them going under and momentarily eliminating themselves as distinct targets as well.

Liz chose to swim to shore. She'd been a strong swimmer in her youth, and in her panic believed it an undoubtedly quicker method than wading. And it was, though it did little to provide the camouflage submerging had provided the others.

The first two bullets missed, but the third ripped into the meat of Liz's calf muscle, stopping her instantly, causing her to cry out and clutch at her wounded leg while desperately trying not to go under.

"*WINNER!*" Harlon yelled with celebration from above.

Ethan and Noah surfaced by the shoreline. Ethan turned when he heard Liz's cry. He immediately rushed back in, diving when the depth of the river hit his waist, and started towards Liz.

"Well, now look at this gentleman," Harlon called. "Reckon you save her and she gives up some of that rich pussy, do you, Ethan?"

Russ had been slowly and quietly wading his way towards the shoreline with Vicky under his arm. When he heard, then saw that his daughter had been shot, Vicky insisted he help Ethan and go after her; she would make it to shore on her own. Russ instantly obeyed, spun, and dove back in.

"Two gentlemen!" Harlon said. "You're not fixin' to get some of that pussy too, are you, Russ? Hell, that's just sick!" He laughed and then steadied the gun on Russ as he swam towards Ethan and Liz.

"*NO!*" Vicky cried from the shoreline.

Harlon lowered the gun and looked over at Vicky. "I was just *kidding*, Mrs. Burk—damn. I know Russ would never do such a thing."

Vicky started turning frantically in all directions. "*HELP!!! HELP!!!*"

Harlon joined in, cupping a hand to his mouth for dramatic effect. "*HEEEELLLPPPP!!!*"

Vicky stopped instantly and stared up at Harlon.

He grinned back. "Where you think you are, Mrs. Burk?"

Russ had since arrived by Ethan and Liz. Started helping Ethan pull Liz to shore. Harlon aimed the gun on them again.

An unlikely and unintentional savior stopped him.

Ida Roy kicked open the screen door with a bang, her nose and mouth still bloodied from Ethan's knuckles. She had not bothered to put her glasses back on when they'd flown off during the fight inside. She was too consumed by blood lust.

Ida snatched the pistol from Harlon's hand and immediately fired down into the water, hitting nothing with the remaining three bullets but continuing to pull the trigger until it clicked empty dozens of times. When her rage allowed a moment's clarity to realize the gun would fire no more, she turned and threw it at Harlon, bent for the chainsaw, and began pulling the cord with senseless vigor, as if it might somehow be useful should she get it started.

Harlon bent and pulled his mother to her feet, her hand still clutching the saw's cord like a fistful of another woman's hair.

"Ma! *Ma!*" Harlon spun his mother by the shoulders so she would face him.

Ida finally let go of the cord, the saw hitting the wooden deck with a clunk. She looked up at her son with a possessed face, started slapping and punching him repeatedly. "*STUPID FUCKING WASTE O' CUM!!!*"

Harlon tucked his chin and absorbed his mother's blows.

Ida went on, words and blows: "*Playing fucking games while your brother sits at death's door!!! Playing fucking games while your mama lay unconscious!!! Playing fucking games while—*" Her rage strangled anymore words, and she bent for the chainsaw, picking it up whole and throwing it at Harlon. He turned and took the brunt of the impact on his arm and shoulder. Ida rushed forward to continue her assault, but Harlon stopped her this time, catching her at both wrists. Ida went berserk, struggling to get free.

"Mama..."

Ida screamed and cursed and squirmed.

"*Mama...*"

Unable to break his hold on her wrists, Ida resorted to kicking her son's shins.

"*Mama!*"

She stopped, panting heavily, staring up at her son, her anger only momentarily paused. "*What!?*"

His hands still gripping her wrists, Harlon flicked his chin out onto the river. "They're gone," he said.

Ida's gaze followed her son's. The river was empty, floodlights illuminating nothing but their own shine on the black water.

Ida's gaze fell back on her son. "No more games, Harlon Roy—" She spit blood at his feet. "Lessen you wanna see this family burn, I suggest you go and ready a boat for you and me...*right fucking now.*"

"Reckon I'll take that big ol' grappling hook of Sam's—far better than any I got," Harlon said.

"I don't rightly care."

"You will when we're fixin' to haul back five bodies."

"Says you, shit for brains." She spit more blood at his feet and then headed back inside, muttering more obscenities under her breath.

Harlon looked out onto the river again. The group was on foot. He questioned if he'd be able to track them in only a boat. Ethan and Noah knew the terrain. Still, a good part of that terrain—the parts that headed back, anyway—rimmed the shoreline, unless you fancied your chances wading in neck-deep swamp that was home to some ornery critters. Ornery critters that might just be extra tempted to investigate a warm and tasty stream of red leaking from the girl's calf, thanks to his deadeye.

He patted his own back with a little smirk.

And then there was the husband and wife. They were old, lacked mobility. They would never be able to chance the swamps either. Ethan and Noah would *have* to take them back on that terrain closest to shore—the easiest way; the safest way.

Harlon suddenly barked out a solitary laugh. *The safest way.*

He left the empty pistol on the deck and headed inside to grab his rifle and scope.

CHAPTER 33

.

"Wait," Liz said. "Wait, I have to stop."

Ethan and Noah stopped. Liz was between them, an arm around each neck as they helped her along. She motioned to the ground, and both Ethan and Noah gently lowered her. Liz sat on her butt and lifted her pant leg. It was soaked through with blood. She winced and moaned as she managed the pant leg to her knee. It was dark, but the moon offered something in this particular spot. It had been like a dark room with a solitary television going thus far in their journey—inconsistent lighting with no discernible pattern. Sometimes good, sometimes dark, sometimes a maddening combination of both, alternating in quick succession, just as your eyes tried to accustom to one or the other.

Now, the TV seemed content to keep the channel on something reasonably bright for a good duration, and everyone got a decent look at Liz's calf. It looked bad, even in the moonlight.

"Is it still bleeding?" Ethan asked.

Liz touched her calf, winced, and brought back a hand painted in blood.

"Jesus," Russ said. "Why didn't you say something, sweetheart?"

"I didn't...I don't know. I didn't think it was that bad."

Russ dropped to one knee. "We need to tie it off." He looked up at everyone. "I need something to tie it off."

Noah, who despite south Florida's infamous humidity, was known to wear two layers to give the impression of more muscle on his young, lanky frame, immediately removed one of his tee shirts and handed it to Russ. Russ took the shirt, wrapped it around his daughter's leg, and began to tie it off above the wound. He stopped suddenly and pulled his hand away as if stung.

"*Goddammit!*" He cradled his damaged thumb.

"I'll do it," Ethan said, dropping down. He took hold of the shirt and started to finish what Russ began. When it was time to cinch the knot, he looked up at Liz with an empathetic wince. "Gotta cinch it tight now."

"Fine," Liz said.

Ethan did, and Liz threw her head back, grimacing at the moon with a hiss.

"One more knot," Ethan said. "To be sure."

Liz said nothing, and Ethan took that as compliance. He cinched a second knot, and Liz moaned.

"Done," Ethan said, getting to his feet. "All done."

"How do you feel, honey?" Vicky asked.

"Dizzy."

They all exchanged looks.

"We need to keep moving," Ethan said. "Tucker might be down, I don't know what the hell is going on with Travis, but sure as shit Harlon and Ida are on our tail."

"He has one leg. She's an old lady. Surely we've got enough of a head start?" Russ said.

"But we're coming up on the river's edge," Ethan said. "I reckon they'll be in a boat. They got spotlights and we'll be visible. Plus..."

"Plus what?"

"Gators tend to congregate near the shore, hoping to catch something stopping for a drink."

Russ looked baffled. "Then why the hell did you take us this way?"

"Because the alternative is to go swimming!" Ethan fired back. "At least this way we see 'em coming."

Russ was out of his element and he knew it. He sighed and conceded with a nod.

"I'm sorry for yelling, Mr. Burk," Ethan said, "but the only other way is in the deep waters of the swamp. In there, we'd be helpless if a gator fancied himself a bite. If we stick to as much dry land as we can, and we move *fast*, a gator won't be bothered with such a chore. They prefer to lie in wait, not chase."

Vicky looked at Russ. "That's exactly what Sam said, remember? Alligators and pythons prefer to lurk and wait?"

Ethan pointed at Vicky. "Exactly right."

"What do we do if one *does* come after us?" Russ asked.

"Not *be* there," Ethan said, gesturing to the forest ahead, urging that they needed to keep moving.

Russ quickly turned his attention down on Liz. "Sweetheart? Sweetheart, can you keep going?"

Liz nodded, looking weary.

Ethan and Noah bent to help her up. Soon, each brother had one of Liz's arms over their shoulder again.

They were about to press onward when the sound of an approaching boat motor froze them instantly.

CHAPTER 34

They were huddled together behind a group of cypress trees. Low to the ground and not even daring to breathe. The boat soon drifted into view on the river, maybe ten yards from where they hid. Russ chanced a quick look. He spotted Harlon and his mother in the boat, waving high powered flashlights back and forth across the black forest, the beams periodically waving their way, but not lingering thanks to the cover of the cypresses. Russ wondered if they should simply wait here. Wait until they drifted by and continued searching down the river. Surely that would give them some kind of edge in eluding them.

Elizabeth.

His daughter was hurt. They'd tied the wound off but she was still losing blood. She needed medical attention far sooner than later. And let's not forget about the wildlife around them. What had Sam said; Vicky reiterating? They prefer to lurk? What better bait could they be for something that lurks if they were to remain still for who knows how long? It's why Ethan insisted they keep moving, and quickly.

Russ decided to chance a whisper to the group, the boat nearly past them now.

"What should we do?" he asked.

"Keep moving," Ethan said.

"But they couldn't see us," Russ said. "They went right by with lights, and they still couldn't see us."

"So?" Vicky said.

"If we keep moving, they *might* see us," Russ said.

"So, what're you saying, we should hang out here all night?" Vicky asked with not a little sarcasm, waving a hand over their surroundings to underline her bite. Russ knew their predicament all too well, but followed his wife's hand anyway. Russ remembered reading an article that stated something to the effect that if people knew what was swimming a mere ten feet from them in the ocean they would never get back into the water. Looking around now, in the black and desolate world of the Florida Everglades, he wondered what was "swimming"

(*"...they tend to lurk and wait, grabbing you when you're not ready."*)

a mere ten feet from them.

And then Ethan's words coming back now instead of Sam's:

(*"...you ask me, the wildlife here—in this house—is far more lethal than anything we're gonna find out there."*)

There was a queer sort of comfort in that. Because that lethal wildlife had drifted past them. Still, did he really want to wait around and put Ethan's theory to the test, give the other wildlife out here a chance to prove their lethality in contrast to the Roy's? The answer was a resounding *hell, no.*

"All I'm saying is that they didn't see us." Russ then pointed. "Look—they're down the river now." In the distance, flashlights continued to move all over the forest like giant fireflies.

"If they didn't see us, then that means they think we've made it farther down the river," Ethan said. "They'll be looking ahead, not back. We can follow and keep track of them this way."

"Follow *them*?" Vicky said.

Ethan nodded. "It's like I said about dealing with a gator on land or in the water. On land you can see them coming, you got a chance. We follow, keep an eye on them, and they'll be like gators on land."

No one responded, but their seemed to be an unspoken agreement with Ethan's logic. He went on.

"We got to keep moving though. I reckon I don't need to explain why again, least of it being the state of Liz's leg."

Russ, his already considerable respect for the fifteen-year-old Ethan Daigle growing by the second, patted him on the back and said, "Okay, son—keep leading the way."

Ida Roy continued to wave her flashlight all over the forest for show.

"Spotted them, did you?" she said.

Harlon was loading his rifle. "I surely did, Mama."

Ida, her anger for her son's previous foolishness hardly gone, allowed herself a little smile. "I want that Ethan Daigle alive. I want his tongue *and* his knuckles floating in my pickle jar come morning, hear?" She touched her wounded face at the hands of Ethan's fists. "You bring him in alive and I do the rest. *I* do the rest."

Harlon slid the bolt home on his rifle, and then peered through the scope a final time. The black woods came alive in his own personal circle of green light. He could see everything. "You got it, Mama."

They started to move again, following the waving flashlights down the river. Ethan and Noah continued to be crutches for Liz while Russ and Vicky followed close behind, periodically stumbling on underbrush, or momentarily pausing as their feet sank into hidden pockets of wet earth, or stopping altogether when the black wilderness around them produced a rustle that sounded too close.

When Ethan, Noah, and Liz stopped suddenly and completely, Russ and Vicky felt a panic stronger than any nearby rustling could bring. They needn't ask why they'd stopped; they could see—or actually, not see.

The flashlights were gone.

They could still hear the distant hum of the boat motor, but the flashlights were gone.

"Are they driving blind?" Russ asked in a frightened whisper.

"Maybe the batteries went out?" Vicky said.

"On *both* lights?" Ethan said.

"What the hell is going on?" Russ asked.

The sound of the boat motor was growing stronger now. They were coming back.

CHAPTER 35

They hurried towards another group of cypress trees and hid behind them, speaking in whispers.

"They're desperate," Ethan insisted. "They're circling back because they think they missed us."

"Coming back without *lights*?" Russ said.

"They know if we can see the lights, we can see them— they're desperate," Ethan said again. "Too bad their boat motor still gives them away."

The antithesis of the deus ex machina stepped in, Ethan's classic jinx far too tempting for it not to...

The boat motor stopped.

The boat drifting silently in the river, Harlon steadied his rifle, eye pressed to his scope. His own personal green-lit world offered so many options. They were well-hid behind the cypress trees, but not *that* well. He could see limbs. No heads, but limbs. And that was good. It gave him an excuse to have a little fun without Mama catching on. *Can't get a bead on their heads, Mama— best wound 'em first, slow 'em down.* She wanted Ethan alive, after all, didn't she?

A grin grew below his scope. He contemplated many limbs...

• • •

"Why did it stop?" Vicky whispered.

Ethan touched Vicky's shoulder. She looked at the boy and Ethan placed an index finger to his lips, gesturing for her to be quiet.

All of them huddled close together, backs pressed tight to the cypress trees. The urge to poke one's head out and peek was maddening.

Would they see anything anyway? Vicky wondered. The moonlight was weak in their current locale. And that meant it was weak for *them* too, didn't it? The psychos were on the river, out in the open, periodically illuminated under the moon the more they drifted, right? If anyone was getting spotted in the dark it would be the psychos. Ethan was right; they were desperate. Let them drift on by. Let the psychos drift on by, back to their psycho home, to their hopefully-bled-to-death psycho brother and son.

She wanted to look. A quick peek. If the psychos were far enough down the river, they could move again. Vicky needed no reminder on the pitfalls of staying put for too long, out here in the Everglades; the nightmarish things of which those that "lurk" might do.

"We need to move," Vicky whispered.

All heads turned to her. Not one face agreed.

"Let me at least look," she said. "If they're far enough down the river, we can move. Ethan, you said it yourself; we don't want to stay put for very long."

Ethan shook his head, pressed a finger to his lips again, frowning this time.

Vicky splayed her hands. "*You* said we shouldn't stay put."

A sudden explosion echoed in the forest, and one of Vicky's splayed hands disappeared.

• • •

The moment Vicky Burk splayed her right hand, Harlon zeroed in. "Gonna have to pull Russ' pecker with your left from now on, lady."

Vicky did not scream. She did not even wince. She merely blinked at the now-jetting stump on her right wrist as though wondering where her hand had gone.

Liz did scream. Russ too. All of them, except Vicky.

And then the explosion of a second bullet. A third. A fourth. Their lethal trajectory whistling by and thumping into the surrounding cypress trees, presenting only two terrifying prospects: run and hope you don't get shot, or stay and hope you don't get shot.

Ethan and Noah made the choice for Liz. They hoisted her up and fled. Liz screamed in protest, wanting to stay with her wounded mother, but Ethan and Noah dragged her away, desperate to find stronger cover.

Russ leapt towards his wife. He gripped her right arm by the elbow, the jetting stump on her wrist merciless in expulsion. Russ could only stare at the wound helplessly; it had been so sudden, so *extreme*. Where to even begin? Tie it off. Just like Liz's wound—tie it off. That was something. With what though? He had no belt. And then he flashed on Vicky's insistence he wear shoes and socks today, despite Russ' desire for sandals. Shoes and socks because who knew what might be crawling around out there, she'd said. He'd eventually agreed, and now, as he quickly removed his shoe to get to his sock, Russ felt an intense surge of anger towards the world; their predicament was apparently not severe enough as is, it needed a grave-pissing bit of irony to boot.

As Russ stripped off his sock and quickly put his shoe back on his bare foot, Vicky's shock began to fade. Her eyes had never left her wrist since the injury, but the once look of confusion and wonder at something possibly too horrific to comprehend, something too instantaneous in it amputation to initially feel, now seemed as though it was becoming something very real.

Her hand was gone.

And when Russ had finally gotten his sock tied tight around Vicky's forearm (his thumb complained constantly, but this only angered and spurred him on) and went to cinch it tight, Vicky finally screamed. And as if the grave-pisser still had a little left in his bladder, Russ was then forced to grab his wounded wife and drag her to the ground where he clamped a desperate hand over her mouth, begging her to keep quiet.

Run and hope you don't get shot, or stay and hope you don't get shot, he thought again. No, that was wrong, wasn't it? They'd shot Vicky with precision; they knew exactly where they were. They could continue to drift in the boat, get a better view—how they were managing that view in the dark, Russ didn't know—and then they would shoot again.

The two terrifying prospects were different now: run and hope you don't get shot, or stay and *wait* to get shot.

They ran.

CHAPTER 36

Liz had resisted the entire way, desperate to get back to her mother and father. Ethan and Noah only continued to pull—sometimes drag—her along, insisting that if they did not keep moving, they were dead.

When Liz managed to pull free from the smaller Noah and throw herself to the ground in protest, the brothers had no choice but to stop and attend to her.

"How the hell could you leave my mother and father!? *My mother!?* She's probably bleeding to death. Did you see her hand!? Or—" She winced at what would have been a dark and clever quip in some fictional circumstance "*NOT!?*"

"Elizabeth," Ethan said, as calmly and quietly as he could, "if we didn't keep moving, we'd all be dead. Now, I know that your folks are hurt and pinned behind those trees, and we *are* going to go back for them—just not the same way we came."

Liz wiped away angry tears. "What do you mean?"

"Harlon and Ida know which way we went; we go back that same way and we might as well be wearing bull's-eyes."

"How could you just leave them there?" she asked again, shaking her head. "You just said if we didn't run we'd be dead. How does that logic not apply to my parents too?"

Ethan's manner was apologetic, yet their predicament demanded curtness. He spoke with a marriage of the two. "It doesn't. My first instinct was to run and to take you with us on account of your leg. You were there, you saw how crazy it was, how fast it all happened. There was no time for thinking, just doing." He stopped for a beat and let out a long, cathartic sigh. "Now, what's done is done—you wanna yell at me some more, or start heading back to your folks?"

Liz slammed a frustrated fist into the dirt next to her. She then extended that same fist upward as an open hand. "Help me up."

CHAPTER 37

Russ and Vicky Burk ran as best they could under their conditions. It was dark, they were deep in the Everglades, and Vicky Burk was missing her right hand—a wound that continued to pulse her life's blood with each passing minute, despite Russ' attempt at tying it off below the wrist. His daughter's wound had been a bullet hole to the calf. It was serious, and his daughter had lost a good deal of blood, but they'd tied that off as well, and done an admirable enough job to stem some of the bleeding so that she could soldier on.

Vicky's fucking *hand* was gone. How the hell did you stem that? Russ had no clue; his medical training came from TV and movies and the odd conversation with doctor friends at parties. As grim as it was for him to admit, his first thought after tying off the wound was to cauterize the stump. Actually set fire to his wife's wrist and let it cook. And then a second—worse?—thought was that if he did set fire to his wife's wrist, the light would give their position away. God, help them.

Vicky finally insisted they stop. Russ spotted a sizeable plot of vegetation by the shoreline and guided his wife towards it. They sat in the damp earth, huddled together, Russ periodically looking out onto the river, hoping beyond hope that the moon's reflection on the river's dark surface would not soon ripple from the motion of an incoming boat...unless of course it was someone else.

Someone else.

How would he know if it was? Simple, dummy—they would have lights, right? Make more noise? The Roys had been as cunning and as calculating as any predator out here—turning off their lights, switching off their boat motor, not allowing its prey to know their whereabouts. But a fisherman, or a boat of locals, or—*of course!*—Sam's employer! Why the *hell* hadn't he considered it before? It was late—surely they would have noted him and his crew overdue by now. They could be out searching this very moment. Perhaps not one boat but two, or three! This was the friggin' Everglades, after all. Sam was experienced, but in such a vast and unpredictable locale, could you ever be too sure? *Especially* with passengers to account for?

Yes, they were out looking for them. Russ was sure of it.

And then, as though spoken from some vindictive part of his psyche, he could actually hear the thought in his ear: *So are the Roys...*

"Russ?"

Russ broke his daze and turned to his wife. "What is it, honey?"

"I'm okay now. Let's keep going."

Russ marveled at his wife's strength. How many would curl into a fetal ball and succumb? If Russ knew his wife—and he did, inside and out, top to bottom—she would make it home, get a robotic hand, return, and choke the living shit out of the Roys with it.

As much as his wife's resolve provided Russ with his own necessary jolt of tenacity, he now questioned Ethan's earlier advice about constantly moving—because no one had ever mentioned the idea of hiding and waiting for Sam's employer to begin their search. Perhaps that was the best course of action? Find a safe spot and wait for the cavalry?

The vindictive psyche spoke uninvited once again: *Safe spot? What the hell do you know about a safe spot out here!? Only a moment ago you conceded to your options being forced on you: run and hope you don't get shot; or stay and wait to get shot. What the hell has changed?*

"Sweetheart," he said. "Sweetheart, suppose we stay here and hide? Sam's employer has got to be looking for us by now, right?"

Vicky looked at Russ. Her eyes were glassy, sickly. Her skin, cruelly heightened by the moonlight, was terribly pale. "We can't hide…" she said, "from anything…" She trailed off as though dozing.

Russ frowned. "What do you mean? Honey, what do you mean?"

She sighed, her voice taking on a dreamy quality. "If we hide, something will find us." Then, like a battered fighter pleading on his stool: "We need to keep going."

"But, honey," he began with a humorless and painful chuckle, "do you know the way? I don't know where Liz and those boys are. We sure as hell can't call out to them…"

Vicky rolled onto her side as though preparing to take a nap, her words contradicting her actions. "We need to keep moving." The bloodied stump on her wrist, stemmed slightly by Russ' sock, seemed to begin pumping anew and with more strength. It seeped into the earth on which she now laid her head.

Was she fading? Christ, the very idea they hide and *wait* while his wife lay horribly bleeding. Moron! Their options had *not* changed; they were, in fact, more resolute than ever, given the extent of Vicky's wounds. They had to keep moving and hope they didn't get shot. If they spotted Sam's employer en route? Oh happy fucking day. Russ would sound the trumpets, get them home safe, buy his wife that robotic hand, and return to choke the piss out of these crazy sons of bitches in prison.

"Sweetheart," Russ said, crawling towards his fetal wife. "Sweetheart, come on." He nudged her shoulder and she moaned. It was a moan he'd heard countless times before when he tried to stir her from the couch at home. The memory singed him and he felt physically sick at his vindictive side's notion that he might never get the chance to do that again.

"*Sweetheart*," he said with more urgency, rocking her harder, eventually rolling her over to face him.

She opened her eyes.

Russ sighed with relief.

"We need to move," she said in the dreamy voice again, the fighter wanting to keep fighting.

"I know, honey. We're going right now."

Russ crouched into a catcher's stance. He placed his good hand under his wife's head to help guide her upright, but went no further. His body froze, rigid with a fear he thought incapable of climbing new heights. A few feet from Vicky's dozing head sat something that had been there the entire time, inexplicably going unnoticed despite its enormity, its serpent body lying in coiled wait.

CHAPTER 38

Vicky looked at her husband. His face, his body, it all seemed to seize up at once.

"What's wrong?" she asked.

Russ did not reply. Did not even look at her. His eyes were fixed beyond his wife, at something behind her.

Vicky turned to see, and Russ gripped his wife's neck hard enough to cease all movement instantly, enough for her to give a small cry.

"What are you—?"

He gripped harder, silencing her save for another pained whimper. When her eyes looked up at him to complain, he did not meet her gaze, *could* not meet her gaze, for he believed that taking his eyes off of it would be tantamount to inviting the python to attack, that they were weak prey, backing down.

"*Shhhhhh...*" Russ said, his eyes never leaving the giant snake, his tone that of a man who was afraid anything above a calculated whisper might trigger a sound-sensitive alarm. "Listen to me, Vicky. I want you to slowly—very slowly—start to get up. But at *no time*, do I want you to turn around, do you understand?"

Russ, hand still cradling his wife's head, felt her neck stiffen.

"Why?" she whispered, taking tonal cues from his voice.

Russ watched the snake intently as he spoke, its seemingly lifeless black eyes catching the moonlight and staring back into his as though it *knew* he was the weaker of the two, that it was only a matter of time until *it* decided when their fate should come.

"Because I said so," Russ decided to say. "Once again: very slowly, I want you to start to get up. At no time do I want you to turn around, okay? Vicky?"

Vicky nodded.

If he was capable, Russ would have exhaled.

Vicky began to get up, slowly and methodically, just as Russ had asked. She did not look behind her.

The python moved.

It did not attack, merely moved a few exploratory inches forward. Russ could not help but flinch away. Vicky turned and looked, and stared into the face of the giant python that was no more than two feet from her nose. She shrieked and flew backwards as though propelled by some unseen force, colliding into Russ, knocking him over, scurrying to her feet, running anywhere that was away.

She ran to the river's edge…where her shrieking had alerted Ida and Harlon Roy to her precise whereabouts.

Where Ida and Harlon Roy then blinded and thus momentarily froze her with light.

Where Harlon had forsaken his rifle in favor of Sam's crossbow, firing the grappling hook and propelling it over and behind Vicky, only to immediately drop the crossbow and grip the hook's rope, jerking it towards him, the iron claw jumping and catching Vicky in the back, all four prongs spearing her flesh, snaring her. Harlon grinned and pulled, dragging Vicky into the shallows of the river towards their boat.

Russ arrived on the scene and cried out, charging into the shallows after his wife. He managed a two-handed grip on one of her ankles and held on with impossible strength.

Harlon continued to grin as he pulled, Vicky screaming in agony as the tug of war between the two men only served to dig the iron hooks deeper into her back. Russ felt his bad hand beginning to give, the anesthetizing effects of the adrenaline ideal for pain, yet useless to a tool that was broken. His bad hand gave out and he screamed with unbearable helplessness as he held on to her ankle with his one good hand for less than a second before Harlon tugged harder, pulling Vicky into deeper water, eventually hoisting her onto the boat.

"Look at what I caught, Russ!" Harlon said, one hand around Vicky's waist, the other under her chin, Ida Roy flashing a spotlight on it all, allowing Russ to see with horrifying clarity.

Vicky's screams were moans now, her injuries draining her by the second. "She's still a floppin', Russ. Never let it be said I'm a man who don't show mercy." Harlon wrenched Vicky's neck to one side, snapping it easily. He let go and she dropped to the boat's floor like dead meat. Harlon brushed his hands together. "Mercy kill, that was. You're welcome."

Russ dove into the water, insane with rage, determined to reach the boat and kill and kill and kill.

Harlon turned to Ida. "Gotta admire his spirit, don't you, Mama?"

Ida laughed.

Russ reached the edge of the boat, crying, screaming, babbling incomprehensible hate. He tried pulling himself onboard. Harlon calmly took hold of his rifle, butt-first.

"Sorry, Russ. I'd like to end it for you, I would. The guilt you must feel for not being able to save your wife must be rough indeed. But we're fixin' to do some fishing for the rest of your group, you see—and we need us some live bait."

Harlon rammed the butt of the rifle between Russ' eyes and knocked him cold.

CHAPTER 39

Once again, Liz had a pair of human crutches—Ethan on her right; Noah on her left. Ethan had suggested an idea of where he believed Russ and Vicky might have fled after Harlon's rifle fire. It would not, Ethan had said while looking at the ground, be the safest of places, but it made the most sense. A straight line.

So they followed it, a slow, cautious hobble through what most eyes and minds would deem a dark and treacherous land chockfull of nature's booby traps, with teeth and without.

"They've got to be hiding," Liz said. "My mother's wound... they shot off her *hand*. She'll have lost too much blood for them to keep going. They've got to be hiding."

"She'll lose blood whether they're moving or not," Ethan said. "Your daddy's clever; he'll know the best bet is to keep moving, lessen they want her to bleed out, or worse yet, have something approach that picked up on the scent of your mama's wound."

Liz closed her eyes for a beat, inhaling deep and then exhaling slow. She eventually glanced up at Ethan. "And what if *they* approached?"

Ethan hesitated.

"My parents don't know this area like you and your brother do. They might have walked right into them."

Ethan shook his head with conviction. "No. Your daddy's too clever. He—"

"*FRESH FISH!*"

They all stopped at once, as though it were rehearsed.

The sound of the boat motor started, the flashlights onboard clicking to life and waving beams in their direction.

"*FREEEEEEEESHHH FIIIIISHHHHH!!!*"

Ethan and Noah immediately began to move, yet Liz dropped her weight, insisting they stay put. She knew this wasn't an attack; it was an invitation.

"*Liz!!!*" Ethan yelled. "*Come on!*"

Liz remained an anchor. "No—let them come."

"*Are you insane!? Get up!*"

Liz jerked her arms free from both brothers and flopped to the ground.

"Suicide!" Noah said to Ethan. "She wants to commit suicide!"

The sound of the boat motor hummed closer, the waving beams of light growing stronger.

"They've got my parents," Liz said dejectedly from her seat on the ground. "That's what this charade is all about."

"*FREEEEEESSSHHHHH   FIIIISSSSHHH!!!!*" Harlon called again.

"Let's go!" Noah said to Ethan.

Ethan looked down at Liz. "Liz!?"

"They want us alive," she said. "It would be too much work for the two of them if they were to kill us here and now."

"So what are you saying?"

"I'm saying they want to bring us back to their place—where we were before."

"*What in the Almighty fuck!?*" Noah yelled.

Ethan scowled at his brother. "You watch your mouth!" Then, squatting next to Liz: "Supposing you're right—they want us alive, back at their place. What then? You think they're just gonna let us go after a spell? You know what they did to Sam...to your boyfriend..."

"GOT YOUR MAMA AND DADDY HERE, LITTLE GIRL! I RECKON IT'S IN YOUR BEST INTEREST TO MAKE IT A FAMILY REUNION BEFORE I START GETTIN' IDEAS...AIN'T THAT RIGHT, DADDY?"

A slight pause and then:

"LIZ, RUN!!! RUN AND—"

The sound of a struggle, a muffled thump, and then silence.

Liz looked hard at Ethan. "I'm staying."

Ethan looked pained.

"Ethan?" Noah said, looking as if he still preferred to run.

"Liz, we get on that boat, and we're as good as dead," Ethan said.

"We don't, and so are my parents. You wanna run, then go. I'm staying."

"We can run and bring back help," Noah said to Ethan.

"They'll all be dead by then," Ethan said.

"So what are you proposing?" Noah asked. "Just said it yourself; we get on that boat and we're dead."

"Maybe Liz is right. Tucker's down and there's been no sign of Travis. One man with a bad leg and an old lady wouldn't wanna have to drag five bodies back to their place—especially now that their bridge is out. They'd wait until we were all inside to do anything; inside by way of our own two feet."

"Or maybe they're fixing to just dumping us in the river," Noah said.

Ethan shook his head. "They went through too much trouble in getting rid of Sam. They're crazy, but they ain't dumb. Dumping us in the river would be asking to get caught."

"LOSING PATIENCE OUT HERE, KIDS!"

Liz started to rise. Ethan helped her to her feet. Liz gave both brothers a final glance, and then started hobbling towards the river.

Ethan looked at Noah. "They killed Mama and Daddy."

"And so, what?" Noah began, "we gonna kill *them*?"

"I'd like to," Ethan said.

CHAPTER 40

Ethan and Noah assisted Liz to the river's edge. The silhouette of the boat was there, waiting, maybe twenty feet out. The high-powered flashlights stopped them just as they reached the shoreline and caused all three to raise a hand to shield the blinding light.

"Ethan'll be first," Harlon called from the boat.

"What do you mean, *first?*" Ethan asked, squinting, still trying to shield the light with his free hand.

"It comes before second, ya stupid boy," Ida said.

Ethan frowned. "I know what it *means*—I'm asking why are you telling us to come one at a time? Liz here is injured badly, thanks to you. She'll need our help swimming out to the boat."

"Who says she's coming onboard?" Harlon asked.

"Huh?"

"*Huh?*" Ida mocked. "Just how stupid are you, boy?"

Ethan frowned into the light again. "Just what is it you're proposing, Harlon Roy? Us standing here by the edge of the river isn't the safest of spots. Suppose a gator comes?"

"Don't you worry, son—right now I got you locked between the eyes. A gator comes and grabs ya and I promise I'll shoot you dead before he gets carried away. How's that?"

Ethan's frown melted. His face, no less blind from the light, now bore a look of exceptional vulnerability. He even touched the spot between his eyes.

"So, come on, Ethan," Harlon called. "Lessen you want those gators to come calling, forcing me to give you a third eye…"

"I ask again," Ethan said, scraping the bottom of the barrel for a show at bravado, "just what is it you're proposing?"

"*He's proposing you get in the fucking boat!*" Ida screamed.

"Mama…" Harlon said, followed by the sound of placating whispers. Then: "Here's how it's gonna be, Ethan—you swim out to us; we take you back to the house; Noah takes the girl back to the house on foot; and we all meet up in exactly one half of an hour. Noah and the girl don't show, and her folks go the way of her boyfriend."

"*What!?*" Liz blurted.

"Couldn't have made it any clearer than that, missy," Harlon said.

"I just told you her leg's in a bad way," Ethan said. "If anyone should be going aboard that boat, it should be her. Let me and Noah make it back to your place on foot."

"Sorry, son," Harlon said, "but you're the only real threat between the three of you. I wanna keep my eye on you the whole time. Plus, who's to say you and your brother don't just run off and leave the poor old Burks, hmmm?"

"*MOM!?*" Liz shouted. "*DAD!?*"

"They're fine," Harlon said. "Just got 'em tied up so they won't hurt nobody."

"Let me see them!" Liz shielded her eyes with a grimace. "Get that damn light out of our eyes!"

"You're not holding any cards here, miss," Harlon said, the blinding light going nowhere. "Now you heard your daddy screaming earlier—you *know* that I got him. You gonna cause trouble when all I gotta do is take my rifle off of Ethan's head and point it at your daddy's? Your mama's?"

"We're not running off," Ethan called. "We'd have done so awhile back if we were fixin' to. Believe me, we had our chance."

"I don't have to believe you, son. I just know what's what and what's now. And I'm telling you, if you don't swim on out here, and if your little brother and that girl don't start heading back to our place on foot—and quickly—then there's gonna be some shootin', and a hell of a lot of breakfast for my babies. Your call, son."

All three exchanged looks.

"What do you reckon?" Noah asked.

"I reckon we don't have *much* to reckon," Ethan said. "We chose to come down here—to back Liz. We gotta see it through."

"You get on that boat, and I'll never see you again," Noah said, fighting back tears. "Not alive, anyway."

Ethan placed a hand on Noah's shoulder. "I don't get on that boat, and you'll watch me drop right here. Says he's got a lock between my eyes—seeing as what he done to Liz's mama's hand, I reckon it's not a bluff." Ethan paused, as if trying to convince himself of his own shaky logic. "Besides, they wouldn't be foolish enough to try anything with me until we were back at the house. Remember, an old lady and a one-legged man don't wanna be dragging bodies far, especially now that they don't have a working bridge."

"So they'll get you back at the house then," Noah said. "What's the difference?"

"The difference is we're buying us some time."

"Like waiting on death row is all it is," Noah said, succumbing to tears now, yet refusing to cry.

"Well maybe the governor will call; see fit to giving us a pardon," Ethan said, squeezing his brother's shoulder and forcing a smile, fumbling for levity at a time when it had no place.

Noah angrily wiped away tears with his forearm. "You still fixin' to kill them?"

"Yes I am," Ethan said.

"How?" Liz asked.

"We shoulda never made it this far," Ethan said. "Maybe we can make it a little further."

"Maybe Mama and Daddy are looking out for us from above," Noah said.

Ethan squeezed his brother's shoulder again. "Damn right, Noah Daigle." Ethan turned to the river and into the blinding light. "I'm coming out!" He started wading into the water.

The sudden explosion of a rifle echoed in the forest and a bullet cut into the water a few feet from where Ethan stood. Ethan's hands shot into the air. "What!? *What!?*"

"Noah and the girl have a longer journey," Harlon said. "Them two will get going first."

"*You could have just said!*" Ethan yelled.

Harlon could be heard laughing. "I just did, son."

Ethan stayed put in ankle-deep water, hands still in the air. He glanced back at Noah and Liz. From the water, his back to the light, he could make them out quite well. His little brother and a wounded stranger, forced to move together throughout a treacherous land made all the more treacherous by the psychotics that pulled their strings. His mother and father were dead. *Murdered.* It was not empty boasting when Ethan said he had every intention of killing Harlon and Ida Roy. He wanted to... dearly. And if Noah was right, if Mama and Daddy were looking out for them from above, it would happen. He would find a way to make it happen.

"Go on," Ethan called to Noah and Liz. "I *will* see you there."

Noah helped Liz up the embankment and away from the river. Soon, even the boat's powerful lights could not find them in the dense forest beyond.

Ethan turned back to the boat. "I reckon they're on their way now—may I continue?"

He could hear Harlon laughing again. "You may."

Ethan swam out to the boat. When he reached the boat's edge, Harlon and Ida clicked off their flashlights and Harlon placed the point of his rifle to Ethan's head.

"Slowly now," Harlon said.

Ethan climbed gingerly into the boat as if he feared tipping it over. When he was completely in, he immediately spotted

Russ and Vicky Burk. Russ was bound and gagged, his eyes his only conduit for a distress neither Ethan, nor Mr. Burk, Ethan guessed, could ever articulate.

As for Mrs. Burk? She was dead. Her pallor, the way her body lay all crooked and wrong; it did not require more than Ethan's fifteen years to know this, and he immediately stood to shout to Noah and Liz, only to have Harlon ram the butt of his rifle into Ethan's gut, doubling him over and gasping for breath. Harlon then brought the butt down onto the back of Ethan's head, pitching him forward into Russ where he crumbled next to him in an unconscious heap, rocking the boat, and causing Ida Roy to both laugh and grip the side of the boat for fear of going over.

Once her legs were steady, Ida made her way over to Ethan's sleeping body, squatted close, and spat brown phlegm into his face. The swelling around her mouth and nose from Ethan's knuckles contradicted her delighted tone as she sang: "*I'm going to have such fun with yoooouuuu...*"

CHAPTER 41

Noah hurried Liz along as fast as he could. It was not easy without Ethan's help—Liz lost her balance on more than one occasion, toppling over into mud or a shallow pool of water or thorny vegetation. This was always accompanied by a painful cry and then a string of expletives…the last one aimed at Noah.

"You need to slow down!" she yelled from the ground, an aching grimace on her face as both hands clutched her wounded calf. "Without your brother, I can't move as fast."

"I'm sorry," Noah said. "It's just…we need to get there first."

Still clutching her calf, still looking annoyed, Liz glanced up at Noah. "I thought this was an unwinnable race on foot. That was the whole point of us getting a head start, wasn't it?"

"It *is* unwinnable," Noah said. "But we're not going straight to the Roy home. We're stopping somewhere along the way."

"What? Where? We don't get there soon—"

"Ma'am," Noah began, looking and sounding older than his thirteen years, "we can't be kidding ourselves. We step in the Roy home without any kind of advantage and we're as good as dead. They got no plans to let us go. Ethan was right about buying us some time. So now we gotta use that time and get us an advantage."

"So, what are you saying? We go to the police?"

"No—we'd never make it back in time." Noah's hands curled into fists. "We need to find Travis."

Liz shot Noah an incredulous look. "What do you mean *find* him? He's probably at the house! Probably tending to his father…"

Noah shook his head. "No…he's a coward…a coward and a liar." Noah's fists clenched tighter. "All of this is his doing, and he knows that. He's weak and stupid and he'll be worried his guilt will make him say something he don't wanna say. So he'll hide until it's all over, avoiding any kind of confrontation." Tears now rimmed Noah's eyes but he refused to blink them away. "My daddy used to say a coward only offers to help after the real work is done."

"You think he's hiding somewhere?" Liz said. "With his father as hurt as he is?"

Noah nodded, fists still clenched, refusing to wipe away the tears that now streamed down his cheeks after the mention of his father. "I *know* he is. And I know where."

"So, what's your plan then?" Liz said. "We find Travis and use him as collateral? Exchange him for your brother and my parents?"

Noah nodded again, finally wiping away his tears and sniffling hard. "Something like that."

"Can we do that? I mean, I'm not exactly in the best of shape…" She pointed at her calf.

"I beat that boy's ass all by myself, with no trouble at all— and that was when I held no grudge." His hands curled back into fists. "I'm sure as *hell* holding a grudge now."

CHAPTER 42

Ethan had been correct about a one-legged man and an old lady not wanting to drag five bodies, especially now that they no longer had a working bridge. Dragging only one had not been without its complaints. And so when Vicky's ankles had finally proven too laborious for Harlon to drag up the embankment and around back, he opted for a simpler, cruder handle: her scalp.

Russ had objected as best he could through his gag, but Harlon offered an alternate view: "At least her head's not banging all over the ground anymore," he'd said as if this truth should have been self-evident, and perhaps Russ should be showing a little more gratitude, thank you very much.

Vicky's body was placed in the cooler along with pieces of Sam, and Ron and Adelyn Daigle. Once again, Russ moaned an objection through his gag, and once again Harlon was quick with a response. "You reckon I should leave her out here to spoil? Have a little more consideration for your missus, Russ."

Once inside, Harlon went to work in tying up Russ and Ethan on the floor in the den. No bedroom this time; he wanted eyes on them constantly. Besides, Tucker was still in his bedroom.

"I'm gonna go see about Tucker," Ida said. "You see to making sure they can't so much as wiggle a toe, you hear?"

Harlon grunted a reply. Ida went into the bedroom, and Harlon went to work on Ethan first. It wasn't a tedious job; both Ethan and Russ had been secured on the boat when they were unconscious. Only their ankles had been cut free to allow them temporary mobility, and so now needed rebinding. Their wrists had remained tight behind their backs throughout. Still, Harlon checked their slack anyway, and when it was Russ' turn, he noticed Russ grimace from something more than mild discomfort. He then noticed Russ' disfigured thumb. He grinned.

"Well, I'll be a son of a bitch," he said. "That's how y'all did it, isn't it? That's how y'all got free." He took hold of Russ' thumb and jerked it back and forth like a joystick. Russ screamed. Harlon kept a firm grip on the thumb as he continued. "Got a buddy of mine who did the same thing to get free of some cuffs. Can do it anytime he wants now. Seems once you pop it the first time, it gets looser and easier every time after. Kinda like a woman, I reckon." He laughed at his own wit, and then his smile faded into mock sorrow. "Aw hell, I'm sorry, Russ. It's too soon to talk about women, ain't it?"

Russ mumbled something into his gag. Harlon removed it.

"Come again?" he asked.

"Fuck you," Russ said. "Fuck you and your family."

Now it was Ethan who garbled an objection into his gag. Harlon let go of Russ' thumb and bent over Ethan. "You have something to add, young man?" He removed Ethan's gag.

Ethan refused to look at Harlon. He squirmed on his side and made eye contact with Russ. "Just be quiet, Mr. Burk. Don't give them the satisfaction."

Ida emerged from Harlon's bedroom and lit a filter-less cigarette. "Let him have his say, boy" she said. "He's just an unfortunate man who got mixed up in all of this. Can't blame him for being as upset as he is." She plucked a fleck of tobacco from her tongue. "That's why we're fixin' to do him quick when it's time." She shuffled towards Ethan and loomed over him. "But *you*, you little fucker…"

Ethan kept his eyes on Russ, acting as though he hadn't heard. "You just stay with me, Mr. Burk—we'll be out of this soon."

Ida laughed. "Yeah—you keep acting like you didn't hear me, boy. You keep acting like you got a prayer in hell." Her body grunted and cracked as she squatted down next to him. She exhaled smoke into his face.

Ethan still refused to acknowledge her. "Just stay with me, Mr. Burk…"

Ida took a deep pull on her cigarette and then immediately pressed the glowing tip into Ethan's cheek. Ethan cried out and unavoidably faced her.

Ida barked a phlegmy cackle. "First hint of pain and his resolve goes right down the shitter! Oh, you *are* gonna be fun, boy."

Ethan quickly turned back to Russ again, the singe on his cheek like a freshly picked scab. Russ' return gaze was sorrow, all traces of recent anger gone the instant the young man had cried out. Gone because he was reminded that while Ethan might have the body and capabilities of a man, to Russ he was a boy; he'd already endured enough emotional and physical hardship for ten men. The prospect that it would continue—get *worse*—and that he could do nothing but watch and feed the boy's delusions that they would somehow escape…

Ida grunted and cracked again as she stood. She walked towards Harlon, who was now loading his pistol by the kitchen counter.

"How's Tucker?" he asked.

"Alive," Ida said.

"Only just?"

Ida nodded. "Done all I can for the time being."

"Need to get him to a proper hospital, Mama."

Ida lit another cigarette. "We will, come morning."

"Assuming he holds out."

"He's a Roy; he'll hold."

Harlon raised a subtle eyebrow at his mother, loaded the sixth bullet, and then spun the chamber and snapped it shut with a flick of the wrist. In a whisper he said, "I know you got it in for this boy, Mama, but we need to do this quick. Can't be playing no games with Tucker in there the way he is. Not to mention it's only a matter of time before Sam's employer reckons something's wrong and starts searching."

Ida scowled at her son. "Can't be playing no games, huh? Harlon Roy, you might be the most hypocritical piece of shit I ever seen. Went to such lengths as to destroy our own damn bridge so you could have your fun, and now you're lecturing me about games?" She shoved her cigarette into his face, stopping the burning tip an inch from his nose. Harlon didn't flinch. "I reckon I might need to be testing *your* resolve."

Harlon calmly took the cigarette from his mother's fingers and stubbed it out on his tongue. He then flicked the cigarette aside, swallowed and said, "Alright?"

Ida snorted. "Hot shit. I'm still taking that boy's tongue."

Harlon conceded with a little nod. "Fine. Travis in there with Tucker?"

"No."

"So where's he at?"

CHAPTER 43

Travis Roy was in the little swamp shack his father had built for him on his sixth birthday. The shack sat off the main river, nestled back against one of many small channels. Travis was not popular in school, but his own little shack helped. A place to read nudie magazines, smoke cigarettes, sneak whiskey—all things too impossible to resist for his classmates, no matter who the host might be.

Noah Daigle had once been one of those boys who saw the shine of the shack's prospects in spite of its dull host. And so now, as Travis sat on the floor of his shack, head down on the magazine in his lap, lanterns in all four corners giving sufficient light, he had a visitor. Two, actually.

"What do you say, Trav?" Noah said. "This here's Liz…"

Travis scrambled to his feet and backed up until he hit the wall. His nervous fingers immediately went to his neck and began twiddling his gator tooth. "What do you want?"

"Seems *your* family's got a hold of *our* family," Noah said, gesturing to Liz. "I reckon a trade's in order."

Travis quickly reached into his pocket and pulled a pen knife. He unfolded the small blade and then held it out in front with a shaking hand. "Get away from me."

"You try anything with that toothpick and you're only gonna get your ass beat worse than before, Travis."

CHAPTER 44

Ida and Harlon Roy sat by the kitchen counter, Harlon laying into a bottle of whiskey, Ida her cigarettes.

Harlon looked at his watch. "Should have been here by now."

"Your idea to make them go on foot," Ida said.

"If I'd told them all to swim out to the boat, that girl would have seen her dead mama. Would have caused holy hell and we'd have been struggling to keep 'em from jumping overboard."

"Could have used your rifle then."

Harlon gestured towards Ethan. "Says the woman who's begging me to keep that one alive so she can have her way with him. Besides, you think we got a mess now, imagine we had to be fishing bodies out of the river. No Tucker—just you and I."

"And Travis."

Harlon snorted and took a swig of whiskey.

"What?" Ida asked.

"Well, he's family, and I love him, but that boy was in the back of the line when they handed out plums. Still not sure Jolene didn't have her a fling with Peewee Herman or the like— only way I can figure Travis being the way he is with Roy blood running through him."

"You don't speak ill of Jolene, you hear? Tucker heard you, he'd split your face in two, even *in* the state he's in."

Harlon took another swig of whiskey.

Ida sneered at the bottle going towards her son's mouth. "And let me tell you, you keep hittin' that whiskey the way you are and it won't take nothing but a tap on that ugly chin."

Harlon smirked and took another swig. He then looked down at Ethan and Russ; they'd been quiet a while. "We're gonna need him, ya know," he eventually said.

"Who?"

"Travis. When this is done, we're gonna need his help cleaning up; I don't care how squeamish he can get."

"He'll help."

"Not if he's not here," Harlon said. "Out in his shack, I bet. Daddy's lying in there dying, and he's pulling his pecker to nudie mags out in his shack."

"Nothing he can do for him. Better he just stays out of the way and leaves his daddy be."

"I guess." He looked at his watch again. "Getting later and later…"

"Girl's injured; Noah's smaller than Ethan; *you* took out the bridge. Give it time."

"Don't *have* much time, Mama." He pointed down at Ethan and Russ. "That there? What you got planned? That's the easy part. It's the *after* that's troubling me. We got a hell of a lot of people to make disappear. Not to mention Sam's boat. Better we get it all done before the sun comes up." He looked at his watch again. "That's about eight hours from now."

Ida lit a cigarette. "Don't need to cut 'em all up and feed them to your flock tonight. Long as we keep them locked and cool like the others—keep 'em from causing a smell—then we should be good for days. Nobody'll get wise, even if they come knocking. That boat on the other hand…you *will* need to get to that tonight."

"And that's a two-man job," Harlon said, his earlier implication about Travis helping evident.

"He'll help," Ida said again.

Harlon pushed away from the counter and headed towards the back door. "Not if he ain't here he won't." He opened the back door and found himself standing face to face with Noah Daigle and Liz Burk. "Well, it's about fucking time."

Harlon grabbed Noah by the shirt and dragged him inside. Liz limped after them, following as quickly as she could.

"Look who finally decided to show, Mama," Harlon said.

Ida echoed her son: "'bout fucking time."

"Dad, you okay?" Liz asked.

"I'm fine, sweetheart."

"Both of you, shut up." Harlon looked at Ida and then gestured down towards Russ and Ethan. "Go get that rope, Mama. We'll get 'em fixed up like these two."

"Why even bother, Harlon?" Russ said from the floor. "You're going to kill us, right? Why even bother?"

Harlon bent over Russ. "Makes me feel safe, Russ. God forbid your daughter and that weaselly little fucker try something while we're marching you outside. Had enough bother for one damn day." He grinned. "How's that for a reason, sir?"

"How's this make you feel?" Noah said behind him. Harlon glanced over his shoulder. Noah's fist was in the air, Travis' gator tooth dangling from it.

Harlon stood upright. "Where'd you get that, son?"

"Where you think?"

Harlon cocked his head with a little smile. "Travis give it to ya?"

"I *took* it," Noah said. "Right after Liz and I made sure nobody would be finding him anytime soon."

"Got him hid do you?" Harlon asked.

"That's right," Noah said, fist and tooth still firm in the air. "Kinda place where one don't wanna be tied up and helpless for too long, lessen they don't wanna end up dinner."

Ida shuffled forward. "And let me guess," she said. "We let everyone go, and you tell us where that place is so we can go and get Travis, that right?"

Noah turned to Ida, wielding the dangling tooth like a crucifix on a vampire. "Right again."

Both Ida and Harlon started laughing. Noah frowned.

"Lord, strike me down right now if that boy ain't more trouble than he's worth," Harlon said.

"Amen," Ida agreed. She turned back to Noah with a little smirk. "No deal."

Noah's defiant face, his puffed-up chest, his firm arm and tight fist wielding Travis' tooth, all seemed to wilt at once. "But...?"

Both Ida and Harlon laughed again.

"*Do it,*" Tucker Roy said from the bedroom door.

All eyes fell on Tucker. He stood at the bedroom door, ghostly white and drenched in sweat. His one hand clutched his wounded abdomen while the other braced against the door frame.

"Of course we were gonna," Harlon said. "Come on, Tucker..."

"My ass, you were. Was gonna leave my only child out there to die."

"Assuming this little shit's telling the truth about what they done," Ida said.

Tucker flicked his chin towards Noah. "And how do you explain Noah having Travis' tooth? My boy would sooner remove his head than the necklace *you* gave him, Harlon."

Harlon showed a brief flash of shame. "Ah hell, Tucker, what do you want me to say?"

Tucker stepped out of the doorframe and towards Harlon, his hand still clutching his abdomen. "I want you to say you'll go get my boy. And I want you to mean it."

"So you're suggesting we let 'em all go, that it?" Ida asked Tucker.

Tucker's stone gaze became an incredulous frown as he turned towards his mother. "To save Travis? Yes. *Hell* yes. What the fuck is wrong with you two?"

Ida glared at her son. "I suggest you watch who you're talking to, son—" she gestured down at Ethan. "Lessen you want me to finish what that *fifteen-year-old boy* started."

"Oh, so he's a boy now is he?" Tucker said. "Thought he was a man, fit for killing."

Ida pushed Harlon aside and got in Tucker's face. "I don't rightly care what anyone calls him. All I *do* care about is watching him bleed."

"At the expense of Travis…"

"Maybe we can have it both ways," Harlon chimed in.

"You can't!" Noah blurted, wielding the tooth again with a look of desperate authority.

Ida, Harlon, and Tucker simultaneously looked at Noah—only Tucker looked as if he didn't want the boy's head mounted on their wall.

"We know, son," Tucker said as evenly as he could. "Tell me where my boy is."

Liz suddenly blurted: "*Where's my mom?*"

CHAPTER 45

"Your mama's safe, girl," Harlon said. "Just needed to compartmentalize, is all."

Liz spotted the faintest smirk appear on the corner of Ida's mouth.

"What the hell does that mean?" Liz said.

"Now who would have figured a cracker like me would know more than a little princess like you?" Harlon said. "Compartmentalize means to divide into groups or" —now it was Harlon who was losing the fight with a smirk— "sections."

"I know what it means!" Liz yelled. She rushed to her father and dropped to his side. "Dad!? Dad, where's Mom?"

Russ could do nothing but cry. Liz shook her bound father, momentarily ignorant to all aspects of his pain. She continued with the same question, the same temporary ignorance, each time louder and with increased force as she shook him, as if she could force away the sickening truth she already knew. "*Dad, where's Mom!? Dad, where's Mom!? Dad, where's Mom!?*"

Russ only continued to cry.

"Not much spine on him, is there?" Ida said.

Liz leapt to her feet and charged Ida, screaming wildly as she attacked. The two locked onto one another's hair and began violently jerking and pulling and winging punches, Liz's youth and rage allowing her to get the better of Ida, eventually dragging her to the floor and sitting atop her chest, raining down punches and obscenities and spit.

Harlon, momentarily stunned by the chaos, hurried towards Liz and his mother and pointed the barrel of the six-shooter at the back of Liz's head.

"*NO!!!*" Tucker cried and dove for his brother, catching his gun hand by the wrist and pointing it towards the ceiling where it discharged once, plaster and dust fluttering down around them.

Harlon and Tucker spun in circles as they struggled with one another—Harlon puzzled and frowning, trying to pull his gun-hand free; Tucker wide-eyed and desperate, trying his damnedest to disarm his brother in his wounded state.

"*What the fuck are you doing!?*" Harlon yelled as they fought.

"*If you kill them, we'll never find Travis!!!*"

"*Get the fuck off me, you crazy bastard!*" Harlon screamed. "*That bitch is gonna kill Mama!!!*"

Harlon's words seemed to have no effect; Tucker continued to fight, the two brothers banging into walls, breaking furniture, the gun discharging once more, this time towards the kitchen, shattering glass and porcelain.

Liz continued flailing down onto Ida with crazed punches, only stopping periodically to grip the sides of Ida's head with both hands and slam it repeatedly onto the wooden floor. Each slam accompanied by spit and venom:

"*CUNT!!*" *Bang!*

"*CRAZY FUCKING BITCH!!!*" *Bang!*

"*CUNT FUCKING CUNT BITCH!!!*" *Bang!*

If Ida was unconscious, Liz didn't know, nor care. She wanted her dead.

Harlon had since changed tactics against his brother, exploiting his injury by firing uppercuts into Tucker's bloodied abdomen with his free hand. Adrenaline could only anesthetize Tucker so much before he began to wilt from his brother's blows, eventually losing his grip on Harlon's gun-hand, allowing

Harlon to pull it free and then slam the weight of the heavy six-shooter onto the side of Tucker's head, knocking him backwards into the bedroom and crumbling to the floor. Harlon quickly followed and stood over his dazed brother, pointing the gun down on him, panting...

"You crazy son of a bitch...I should do it...I should fucking well do it."

Tucker looked up in a stupor, but still with enough wits to mutter: "You gotta find my boy...please...he's all I got left..."

Harlon sneered and then spit into the corner. "You sicken me sometimes, little brother." He lifted his boot high and then stomped down onto Tucker's face, knocking him out cold.

Quickly popping the gun barrel of the six-shooter, spotting the four remaining bullets, and then slamming the chamber back with a flick of his wrist, Harlon hurried out of the bedroom to help his mother.

Everyone was gone. Everyone except for Ida, of course. She lay moaning on the floor, her face a battered mess, her consciousness in and out like Tucker's in the bedroom.

Harlon kicked over a chair. "God *damn* if I don't hate when this happens!"

CHAPTER 46

Noah had put Travis' pen knife to good use while Harlon and Tucker were busy fighting, and of course, while a possessed Liz was bouncing Ida's head off the living room floor. There had simply been too much chaos for anyone to notice. Even Russ hadn't noticed at first. Noah dropping low and cautiously duck-walking over towards his brother, cutting his wrists and ankles free, the two of them then quietly nudging Russ to snap from the spectacle of his daughter's fury that held his attention completely.

Once Russ had been cut free, they'd received reparations from the total antithesis of the deus ex machina that had all but buried them earlier: Harlon and Tucker's fight had spilled over into the bedroom, giving all three the precious time and solitude they needed to pull Liz off Ida and hurry out the back door.

Ethan took lead, hurrying everyone around the perimeter of the Roy house, periodically sloshing through the shallows of the swamp, periodically catching an ankle on the twisted undergrowth. Still, they managed a tight group of four, Russ helping his limping daughter, Ethan constantly checking over his shoulder to ensure they were keeping up.

It was only when Ethan started leading them down the embankment, closer to the main river's edge, and where the very end of the Roy bridge had once been, that Russ voiced his concern.

"What are you doing? We should keep to the woods! They spotted us from the river last time!"

Ethan didn't reply. He didn't need to. The dark, the surrounding wilderness, the frenetic adrenaline of the escape; it had impeded Russ' sight. But now as they approached, Russ saw it clearly. And when Ethan began untying the line and said "Lessen they feel like swimming, they won't be doing shit from the river without this," Russ wanted to kiss the boy.

They all piled onto Harlon's boat.

CHAPTER 47

Harlon helped his mother to her feet and walked her towards the kitchen counter. They took a seat.

"That's twice... *twice* they got away," she said, wiping the blood from her face.

"I know it, Mama," Harlon said.

Ida turned and spat blood on the floor. "Don't deserve to be calling ourselves Roys."

Harlon looked away.

Ida wiped more blood from her face and then winced as she touched the back of her head. "Crazy little bitch...had the devil's strength in her."

Harlon said nothing.

Ida glanced at the bedroom. "Tucker still out?"

Harlon swigged from the whiskey bottle. "He's out. Whether it's from me stomping his stupid head into the ground or from losing more blood, I don't know—nor do I rightly care right about now." He placed an exploratory eye on his mother after that last comment, to gauge her reaction.

He was delighted when she spat more blood and said: "Nor me."

Harlon grabbed his rifle from the kitchen. "I say fuck Tucker and fuck Travis and especially fuck those walking dead people out there. Because that's what they are, Mama—walking dead people." He placed the six-shooter on the counter, in front of his mother.

"Ain't doing much walking, boy. I reckon you heard them taking your boat?" Ida said.

"I heard." Harlon finished the bottle of whiskey in three long gulps then violently whipped the empty bottle against the wall, shattering it completely. He was drunk. Worse still, he was *blood* drunk. He wanted everyone dead. Consequences for extremities meant nothing to him anymore. Just dead. He flicked his chin at the pistol on the counter. "Grab that gun, Mama…" And then towards the closet door: "And then grab something to keep you warm. Boat *I* got in mind can get a little breezy."

CHAPTER 48

They cruised down the river in Harlon's boat. Ethan sat closest to the stern, driving; Noah by the bow, lighting their way with one of Harlon's flashlights; and Russ and Liz sat huddled together in the middle of the boat in a tight embrace—Russ would not let her go.

Even if Harlon hadn't left the keys (and he had—no worry for outsiders venturing this deep into the swamp, and surely no worry for locals being stupid enough to steal Harlon Roy's boat), Ethan was savvy enough to get the outboard motor running with spit and fingers. He'd been prepared for both possibilities, hoping for the former in the name of speed, and experiencing something as close to relief as he was capable when he got the latter and saw those keys sticking out of the outboard motor like a prize.

Noah glanced back at his brother. "Looks like a straight shot for the next hundred yards or so, Ethan. Kinda hard to tell so late at night. Reckon I should use another light?"

Ethan, one hand behind him as he steered, squinted ahead and then shrugged. "Couldn't hurt, I suppose."

Noah bent and came up with a second light, but not before flashing one of the powerful beams on an endless length of dark rope coiled up in the corner that made him jump.

"Fuck me!" he blurted before instantly apologizing. "Sorry… looked like one hell of a big cottonmouth…" Noah then traced the light over the coil of dark rope towards the large grappling hook and crossbow it was fixed to. "Well, look at this," he said, picking it up.

Ethan leaned forward at the stern to get a look. "Daddy had one of those when you were little. Used it for dragging the river. Didn't have no bow like that to fire it though."

"Looks like something Batman might use," Noah said.

"Could we please stop talking about it?" Russ said.

Neither boy offered up a reply. Russ' request seemed good enough for them. They motored on in silence for another couple of minutes.

Noah finally spoke. Two flashlights now held in front, he glanced back at his brother. "Helping at all, Ethan?"

"You tell me."

Noah shrugged. "I suppose."

"If nothing else, it'll alert people to our presence," Ethan said.

"Unless it's the wrong people," Liz muttered, her head resting on her father's shoulder.

Russ immediately began running a hand over his daughter's head. "You know, if it wasn't for you, sweetheart, we wouldn't be here," he said. "You saved us."

Liz said nothing.

"He's right," Ethan said. "If it wasn't for you, Noah never would have been able to cut us free."

"I just saw red," Liz said. "I saw my mom…" She choked on "mom" and started to cry into her father's shoulder.

Russ pulled her in tight.

But then as quickly as she'd started, Liz stopped. She pulled away from her father and looked at Ethan, then Noah, desperately wiping away tears.

"Jesus, what the hell is wrong with me? I am so, *so* sorry, guys," she said.

Ethan held up a hand. "One tragedy is no worse than the other."

Liz shook her head. "No…what you poor boys must be going through…"

"It's alright," Ethan said.

"No—it's *not*. What's going to happen now? What are you boys supposed to do *now*?" Liz asked, head going back and forth between Ethan and Noah.

"Now?" Ethan said. "Now, I'd just like to get us to safety, is all. We can work the rest out after that."

Russ shook his head with a short smile and then looked at Ethan with an admiration he felt for few men, let alone a fifteen-year-old boy. "You're what we call an 'old soul,' son." He then turned and looked at Noah. "You too, Noah. And as to what we do *after*? I can assure you, I'll be taking care of both you boys, one way or the other."

Had such words been uttered by a Mr. Russell Burk to a different pair of boys up north, such words would have been met with salivating grins and dollar sign-eyes. Ethan and Noah merely nodded and thanked Russ—their thank yous more obligatory than hopeful. And again, Russ allowed each boy a glance of admiration. He did want to help them when this was over (scratch that, he *would* help them), but how? Talk about different worlds. Mere money seemed to offer no consolation. And Jesus, would it to anyone who'd witnessed and endured what these boys had? Sadly, Russ could think of a few cockroaches he'd dealt with in his day where it surely would. But not these boys. Money would almost assuredly be involved somehow, but not directly. He only needed to find the appropriate method of delivery. So why not ask?

"You know, I'm serious, boys," Russ said. "It would mean a great deal to me, to Liz too, I'm sure—" He looked at his daughter who immediately nodded back. "If I could provide for your future somehow." He then gave a little shrug and passively reiterated: "Somehow…"

"We need to finish school first, Mr. Burk," Ethan said. "It was important to Mama and Daddy that Noah and I finish high school."

"Where will you live?" Liz asked.

Ethan shrugged. "My Aunt Gina maybe."

Noah pulled a little face. Russ spotted it.

"You don't like your aunt, Noah?" he asked.

Noah kept his eyes on the river ahead. "She's okay."

"What if you boys lived with me?"

Ethan chuckled, but there was no trace of humor on his face. "I don't think so, Mr. Burk."

"Why not?"

"How do you reckon two boys like Noah and me would fit in at one of them schools up north?"

"You could stay here, in the school you're in now. I'll drive you—every day. If there's some bullshit residence law to get around, we will."

"Kids at school would give us holy hell they found out we were living up north," Noah said.

Ethan nodded. "That they would."

"Well, there's got to be *something*," Russ said. "We're not just going to forget about you boys once we get home."

"Mr. Burk, we've still got a bit of a ways to go. I appreciate all that you're offering, but right now I think we should just—"

"I'd like to see Mama and Daddy get a proper burial," Noah said.

Everyone stopped.

Noah's eyes stayed on the river, both flashlights out in front, but the tightness in his voice suggested he was fighting back tears. "I don't know where they are right now...Harlon Roy said they were gonna feed them to his gators..." He paused, the tightness in his voice now cracking. He quickly cleared his throat and shook his head, this time offering his profile to the group. "If they're still...I don't know...*around*...I'd like to find them and give them a proper burial. Even if they're not around…just a proper burial." He turned completely now and looked at Russ. "I guess that's something you could do."

Without hesitation, Russ said, "If it can be done, it will be done. You have my word." He turned and looked back at Ethan and said again: "You both have my word."

Ethan only nodded a thank you in return. He too was trying not to cry.

CHAPTER 49

Harlon's rifle lay across his lap as both hands operated the controls to Sam's boat. "Been awhile since I drove one of these things," he muttered.

Ida, standing at the bow, glanced back at her son up high in the driver's seat. "Just keep it quiet and steady—" She pointed to the giant fan behind him. "Don't gun the damn thing or they'll hear us a mile away."

"Who cares? Not like they'll be able to outrun us. I reckon this thing can do sixty."

"You wanna race 'em or kill 'em?"

They continued cruising silently down the river, Ida like a hawk at the bow, desperate to spot any light up ahead. They were driving seemingly blind through the black swamp, refusing to use the plentiful spotlights fixed to Sam's boat. But much like the drunken old man who knew the road home no matter how pickled, so too did Harlon when it came to the river. And so too was he drunk. Drunk and eager. It was taking too long.

"Need to kick it up a notch, Mama. We'll never catch them at this speed."

"Don't need to catch them. Just spot 'em."

"Never spot them at this speed either."

She glanced back at her son with a stern eye. "Fine—but keep it in check; I don't feel like going overboard, you drunken fool."

Harlon hit the gas.

CHAPTER 50

"How are we doing, Noah?" Russ asked.

Noah kept the flashlights on the river. "Fine, I guess." He looked back at Ethan. "How much farther you reckon?"

Ethan shook his head. "I don't know—it's so damn dark. Tough to get your whereabouts when you can only see ahead a little at a time."

"But we're going in the right direction?" Russ asked.

"Far as I know. Truth be told, I'm hoping we spot someone before we find a good place to stop."

"What do you mean?" Liz asked.

"Well, I guess it's kinda like being lost at sea on a raft. Better a big old ship comes along to rescue you than having to make it to shore on your own, you know?"

"But are we really lost at sea?" Russ said. "I mean, you know these parts—this is your home."

Ethan shrugged. "If you hit a big switch right now and turned on the sun, I'd agree with you. But the dark changes things. A safe place during the day might not be so at night." Ethan killed the motor for a moment. "Listen…"

The motor had been a muffler to a cacophony of life echoing all around them. Life they could not see. Calls and howls, clicks and croaks, and perhaps what Ethan was really after, the occasional sound of splashing. Sometimes light, sometimes heavy, sometimes a thrashing, but always so frighteningly close. Russ could not help but flash on the python that had sent Vicky running towards the water. How something so big and so deadly could have been so damn close the entire time they were hiding. A pang of anguish for his wife was unavoidable, and suppressing it without crying out syphoned from the deepest tank of his resolve.

Ethan looked at Russ. "Not to mention we still probably got a couple of loonies chasing after us." He shrugged again and gave a sad little smile. "I think I'd rather be rescued by the big old ship, wouldn't you, Mr. Burk?"

Russ returned an equally sad smile.

Ethan turned the motor back on, and the ambient noise of life was muffled once again—as was the distant sound of a fan boat approaching.

CHAPTER 51

Mother and son saw the lights in the distance. And they were on quite possibly the straightest stretch of river they could have hoped. Over a hundred yards at least. No chance of them veering off into another channel in an effort to hide. They were fucked.

Harlon killed the motor. Momentum carried them down the river as he leaned forward in the seat, rifle up and scope pressed to his eye. The dark river became the familiar green circle of light. But goddamn if it wasn't a little fuzzy. He pulled his head away, shook it vigorously, and then pressed his eye into the scope again. He could see the boat. See the passengers on the boat. If only they would keep still.

"No shooting off hands, you hear?" Ida said from the bow. "You do it right and make 'em all count. Lord knows who's on the river now, looking for this damn boat."

Harlon gritted his teeth. His green world was still fuzzy, the green silhouettes of the passengers still swimming in his sights. If only they would just keep still...

Ida turned and faced her son. "No games, Harlon! Do it quick and do it right!"

Harlon gritted his teeth below the scope. "Shut up..."

"You drunken fool!" Ida scolded. "You're seeing fuckin' double, aren't ya!?"

"Shut up! I can't fucking concentrate with you carrying on!"

Ida spat and turned back to the river.

So fuzzy...everything all blurred together. If only he had a damn rocket launcher that required little accuracy, he'd blow them all out of the fucking water—

Harlon pulled his eye away from the scope. He then started to grin. Sometimes he was just too damn clever for words.

He stuck his eye back on the scope but did not aim at anyone. He had a better target in mind.

"Looks like we got a nice long stretch of river up ahead," Noah called to Ethan from the bow. "Just keep it straight."

"Can do," Ethan said, switching the outboard's tiller from one hand to the other so he could stretch.

An explosion—an all too familiar explosion—echoed throughout the forest.

Liz screamed. Russ grabbed his daughter and pulled her to the floor of the boat. Noah and Ethan immediately followed, the boat's propeller stopping the moment Ethan's hand left the tiller.

"*Who's hit?*" Ethan whispered loudly. "*Who's hit?*"

All of them, flat to the floor, patted their bodies and checked for wounds as the idling boat slowly drifted to a stop.

"I'm fine," Liz said.

"Me too," Russ said.

"Noah?" Ethan asked.

"I'm okay."

"Could it have been someone else?" Russ whispered. "A hunter?"

Another explosion echoed. Everyone flinched and pressed themselves tighter to the boat floor. Something had hit them; Ethan heard it. He risked a glance behind them and spotted a large bullet hole by the stern of the boat—inches from the outboard motor.

"Oh Christ," he said.

"What is it?" Russ asked.

"He's aiming for the motor. He's trying to blow us up."

CHAPTER 52

"**D**id ya get 'em!?"

Harlon ignored his mother and fired again. He saw no result in the distance. He gritted his teeth and fired again. Nothing.

"Fucking hold still…" he muttered, cursing his drunken vision.

He fired again. Still nothing. "*FUCK!*"

"*You drunken waste! You're not hitting a fucking thing, are you!?*"

He fired two more shots in frustration, neither of them anywhere near their mark. His mother continued to chastise his drunkenness, his uselessness. His green-lit world was becoming red. When he saw the fuzzy silhouettes leap from the boat and begin to swim ashore, he was seized by an even deeper state of rage and panic. If they got to shore and started on foot, he would never catch them. Couldn't hit a stationary boat motor, no fucking way was he hitting a bunch of lean silhouettes as they fled. No fucking way in *hell* once they hit the cover of the forest.

"Fuck this." Harlon hit a switch, and Sam's boat exploded with light like some wild night-ride out of an amusement park. He was about to go as fast too.

• • •

Everyone's belly button remained flat to the boat floor.

"What do we do?" Russ asked. "*What do we do?*"

Another shot echoed. Everyone flinched.

Ethan peeked towards the stern, still only the one hole. "We need to get out," he said.

"Out where?" Liz asked.

"In the water."

Another shot fired. Another group flinch. Another miss.

"*Are you crazy!?*" Liz said. "I'm not going in that water!"

"And if we stay put?" Ethan said. "How much longer until he stops missing?"

Two more shots in quick succession. Two more misses.

"Why does he keep missing?" Noah asked. "Managed to shoot Mrs. Burk's hand off." Then a quick apologetic glance at Russ. "Sorry."

Russ said nothing.

"Maybe he's too far behind," Ethan said. "Either way, it's only a matter of time until he *don't* miss. We need to get in the water now."

"Oh God…" Liz said. "There could be anything in there…"

"Don't think. Just jump in and swim like hell. *Go!*"

Russ and Liz jumped together. Then Noah. Ethan was ready to go when the fan boat lit up in the distance. He spun wide-eyed, fear catching in his throat. The boat was maybe a good one hundred yards down the river. The lights meant Harlon had abandoned his game of stealth and was now planning to approach. And in Sam's fan boat, approach quickly. Ethan spun back towards the river's edge. All three were determinedly swimming to shore, not daring to look back. They were almost there. What then? What then when they *all* got to shore and Harlon was close once again? Close enough not to miss this time?

"*I'll* fucking tell you what," he muttered, grabbing the crossbow and grappling hook, and then diving overboard.

• • •

"Hold on to something, Mama," Harlon said.

"Just what the hell do you have in mind!?"

"Grab hold of something, I said."

Ida refused to sit. She gripped the railing tight with both hands and widened her stance. "I swear to Christ if they get away, Harlon Roy..."

"They ain't going nowhere, Mama."

Harlon hit the gas. The boat roared and shot from its idling spot, speeding towards the empty boat and its abandoning passengers ahead.

Russ, Liz, and Noah made it safely to shore. They now stood fidgeting, anxiously waiting for Ethan to join them—all eyes on the fan boat's lights in the distance; eyes back on Ethan swimming; eyes on the fan boat; eyes back on Ethan...

Russ was surprised Ethan was moving through the water as slow as he was. If anything, he should be the fastest swimmer of them all. He wondered if the boy had been hit by one of the bullets. When Ethan came closer, he noticed why the boy's stroke had seemed lumbering and awkward. He was carrying something with him as he swam.

Finally to shore, Ethan hurried towards the group, carrying what Russ could now see was the crossbow with hook and rope that had snared his wife.

"What are you doing!?" Russ asked, gesturing to the crossbow. "Why did you bring that!?"

Ethan ignored him and began pushing the group towards the trees. "Go towards the trees and take cover. Keep low. Noah, you take lead."

"Where are *you* going?" Russ asked.

Ethan ignored him again. "*Go on, Noah!*"

Noah began urging Russ and Liz to follow him up the embankment. They followed half-heartedly, eyes stuck on Ethan who was now sprinting down the shore line—towards the advancing fan boat in the distance.

Harlon had no idea how fast they were going, but it was fast enough to blow his hair back and make him squint through the breeze. Fast enough to cause Ida to widen her stance and grip the rails tighter before shooting a quick glare back at her son. He thought of the possibility that some would struggle to swim to shore. The girl especially; her leg was injured. Suppose they would still be in the water when he arrived? He could run the fuckers right over, take their heads clean off.

He all but squealed at the thought and cranked the throttle more so. Ida screamed and cursed her son as she nearly lost her balance. He didn't care. He could finally see his boat in the distance with his naked eye. Too far to spot swimmers just yet, but they were getting closer.

Panting and dripping wet, Ethan reached his mark along the shoreline. He'd left the group a good ten yards behind. The fan boat powered forward maybe fifty yards ahead, closing fast. Faster than he'd hoped. But why wouldn't it? Harlon had no handheld flashlights like they'd had, only illuminating so far, forcing them to maintain a cautious speed. The fan boat was adorned with spotlights, giving him vision for several feet, hell, maybe even yards at a time. Harlon *could* afford to gun it.

He needed to work fast.

Ethan set the crossbow and hook down then took hold of the thick coil of rope fixed to the iron hook. He ran it a few feet up the embankment to the mark he'd spotted before sprinting away from the group: a fallen cypress. A damn big one too. Ethan immediately began looping the coil of rope around the thickest part of the fallen cypress he could reach. He wanted two passes, but Harlon was closing in. He could hear him; see the lights in his peripheral vision. Ethan's hands shook and his heart pounded in his head and neck and chest. One pass would have to do. One pass or he wouldn't make it.

Ethan knotted the loop several times, pulling the rope on the final knot for all he was worth. The boat's rumble, the lights, all frighteningly close, faster than he could have ever fathomed. The boat's speed would make his goal that much more diffi-cult...but the reward that much greater.

Ethan hurried down the embankment and reclaimed the crossbow. He gave it a quick study to ensure the iron claw was loaded.

The fan boat was almost upon him now, speeding towards the discarded boat twenty yards ahead. Harlon could not see him; of this Ethan was certain. His speed was too great to suggest otherwise. Harlon was heading straight for the boat, straight for the group. His rage and blood lust giving him tun-nel vision.

Ethan steadied the weight of the bow on his hip, aimed it as straight as his straining muscles would allow.

Shoot before it appears straight ahead. Before. The boat is going too fast, the hook's trajectory will be too slow; it will sail right past them. Shoot before. *Before.*

His pulse pounded in his ears like drums, all but trumping the fan boat's monstrous engine. His peripheral vision was now his only guide.

It was nearly there. Ten yards tops. It would pass him if he blinked.

Shoot now.

Now.

NOW!

Ethan fired.

Ida was screaming—*shrieking*—for her son to stop. The fan boat's speed was so great she had resorted to gripping the rail-ing with her forearms, her feet constantly shuffling in place, desperate for better balance.

Harlon heard none of it; he was getting too close to his prey. He hoped there were stragglers still in the water. Hoped that he would run one over, just as he'd envisioned. Run *two* over. If he felt he'd missed he would cut it inches from his boat and create a disorienting wake that would toss them, drown them, buy him time to *take* his time.

Ida shrieking louder.

Harlon grinning wider.

He was heading straight for his boat, and he hit the throttle more so, his drunkenness causing him to abandon all reason. More speed meant more dead. He would plow right through his fucking boat if he had to.

More speed, more dead.

Ida shrieking in absolute terror...

Harlon grinning with maniacal glee...

The boat's giant fan roaring on approach like a primordial beast...

Almost there, almost there, almost there—

Something big shot across Harlon's field of vision, sailing past him. A bird?

Something suddenly on his lap now. Rope?

Rope now sliding off his lap with furious speed, burning his thighs. And then the giant bird again, appearing out of nowhere as it clamped onto his side with impossible strength, what felt like steel talons sinking into his flesh and bone, ripping him from the driver's seat, tossing him thirty, forty feet into the night sky.

The fan boat flew towards Harlon's boat unmanned, Ida Roy at the bow shrieking uncontrollably, the two boats colliding, Ida being pitched from the fan boat's bow, her frail body sailing through the air until landing on a bed of rocks in the shallows, the impact shattering everything, killing her instantly.

The fan boat's size and speed caused it to hop Harlon's boat and slam to shore, its momentum carrying it up the embankment several feet, the giant fan eventually slowing to a stop until it was suddenly very quiet.

Russ, Liz, and Noah watched it all from a safe distance farther up the embankment, each of their faces painted the same picture of disbelief.

Ethan was busy with something farther up shore.

CHAPTER 53

Ethan grunted as he pulled the rope, and thus his catch from the river. Russ, Liz, and Noah arrived at his side just as Ethan dragged Harlon's body to shore. His body was still impaled on the iron grappling hook. He was also still alive, coughing and sputtering both blood and water.

Ethan rolled Harlon onto his back with his foot, bent and ripped the big hook from Harlon's body. Curiously, Harlon did not cry out. Instead, he went to move but could not. Only his head was capable. It whipped left and right, up and down on the muddy shore with interchanging expressions of anger and fear.

"What the fuck is...?" His head flopped left. "Why can't I...?" His head flopped right. "*Why can't I move my fucking arms and legs!?*" He spat more blood.

Ethan tossed the iron hook aside and then looked over at Russ. "What do you reckon, Mr. Burk?"

"Spinal cord injury most likely," Russ said.

The anger on Harlon's face was now replaced entirely by fear. A frantic fear. "I need a doctor," he said. "You need to take me to a doctor."

Ethan laughed. "We *need* to, huh?" He then looked down shore and fixed on the fan boat, where it had hopped up onto the embankment. "Think all four of us can drag that back into the river?"

Everyone, Harlon too, looked toward the fan boat in the distance.

"I think so," Russ said.

Ethan nodded. "Let's get a move on then." He huddled everyone together and began to walk them towards the boat.

"*Wait!*" Harlon cried. "*Wait, wait, wait, wait, wait...!* You can't just leave me here, boy!"

Ethan glanced back at Harlon. From the knees on up his body lay on shore; only his feet, or that is, foot was submerged—his prosthetic lower leg was gone. "You won't drown," Ethan said.

"You *know* that's not what I meant, boy!"

Noah chuckled behind Ethan. Ethan turned and saw Noah pointing out on the river. "His leg!" Noah said with delight.

Sure enough, Harlon's prosthetic leg was floating on the river.

Now Ethan laughed too. "Well, there's some good luck for you, Harlon," he said. "Not that you'll have much use for it anymore."

Harlon ignored the quip, looked as if he didn't even care; something far more serious was weighing on his mind. "You can't just leave me here, boy—you know what'll happen."

Ethan glanced down the shoreline, back the way they'd came. In the distant dark he could just make out the long thick shapes gathering on the shoreline, some emerging from the water, some crawling down the embankment. Likely, they'd scattered from the chaos of the crash. Now their actions suggested curiosity.

Ethan turned back to Harlon and found that his head was flopped in that same direction, the moonlight catching his increasing fear like a spotlight.

"What was it you said before?" Ethan said. "Fresh fish?"

Liz stepped forward and spit on Harlon.

Harlon started nodding emphatically. "Fine, fine, I deserve that, I deserve that...I deserve all of it. Get me out of here and I'll tell the police everything, I swear...everything."

Ethan glanced back down the river's edge towards the congregation of alligators in the distance. He could hear their faint hisses and growls as they jockeyed for dominance among their flock, yet they continued to keep a cautious distance—for now.

Ethan turned back to the group and huddled them together again, gesturing towards the fan boat. "Let's go."

"Finish me off then!" Harlon said.

"Not much in the mood for favors right now, Harlon," Ethan said over his shoulder as they started towards the boat.

"You can't leave me here like this, boy! Finish me off goddammit! *Finish me off!*"

They arrived at the fan boat.

"*I'm sorry, okay!? I'm sorry! You can't leave me here to be eaten alive!!!*"

All four managed to drag the fan boat down the embankment and into the water. Liz spotted Ida Roy in the distance. She lay motionless, face down in the shallows. Liz pointed to her and asked: "Think she's still alive?"

"Not unless she's breathing water," Ethan said.

"*You can't leave me like this!!! Please!!! PLEEEEAAAASSSE!!!*"

They all climbed aboard as if they heard nothing. Ethan climbed into the driver's seat. "Everybody good?" he asked.

They all nodded.

Ethan gave one final glance back at Harlon. He smiled a little. The gators were getting closer.

"*I'M SORRY!!! I'M SORRY!!! I'M SORR—*"

Ethan started the engine and Harlon's shouts went away.

After only five minutes down the river, the big ship came along and rescued them. Ethan finally broke down and sobbed in Russ' arms.

CHAPTER 54

Travis paced back and forth by the window of his shack, willing the sun to rise. If he'd still had it, his fingers would have been anxiously working on the gator tooth that once hung from his neck. No longer. In exchange he sported a sore nose crusted with blood and what felt like a sprained wrist. All courtesy of Noah Daigle.

He was not to move from his shack until sun up. That's what Noah had told him. Don't move or else.

So Travis had stayed put. He was not keen on a third beating at the hands of Noah Daigle. Why did Noah take his necklace from him though, he wondered? He was going on about something Travis didn't understand. A trade? A *family* trade? What did that mean? He'd been scared and confused and pulled his pen knife as a threat, but this only seemed to anger Noah further. The knife was violently wrenched from his hand and a few good whacks that had Travis counting stars had been his reward for posing such a hollow threat. That and his prized gator tooth ripped from his neck along with his pen knife tucked into Noah's back pocket for the keeping.

The light was beginning to gray. Sun up was close. Travis paced faster. He wanted to go home more than anything. He wanted to see his daddy, to see if he was feeling better. Harlon and Meemaw were probably taking good care of him, but

Travis wanted to be by his daddy's side, ask his daddy why Noah would want to steal his necklace and say all those strange things he'd said about trading families. He didn't want to trade families. He liked his family.

The gray dissolved. Morning light poked through openings in the swamp that foliage allowed. Travis hurried home.

CHAPTER 55

"Daddy?" Travis called the moment he stepped inside. "Daddy?"

"Travis!?" Tucker Roy's voice was weak and strained, but the surprise of hearing his son's voice had given it a momentary boost. "In here, son! I'm in here!"

Travis followed his father's voice to Harlon's room. Tucker was slumped in the corner, his hand pressed to his stomach, the bottom half of his shirt long since soaked through with blood. Excessive paleness from blood loss heightened the coloring of the wounds on his face, wounds given to him by both the Daigle boys, and his own brother.

"Daddy..." Travis said at the door, his voice low and soft with shock. "Daddy, you look *worse*."

"Get in here, son." He grimaced as he patted a spot next to him on the floor. "Come sit by me."

Travis knelt next to his father. "Why do you look worse, Daddy? Didn't Meemaw take care of you?"

Tucker ignored the question and instead asked: "How did you get free?"

Travis frowned. "Free from what?"

"Noah Daigle and that girl come here with your necklace, saying they got you tied up somewhere."

"Well, yeah, Noah come by my shack and took my necklace...took my knife too."

Now it was Tucker that frowned. "And...?"

Travis shrugged. "And then he warned me to stay put 'til the sun come up."

"That's it? They didn't take you somewhere? Tie you up?"

Travis shook his head.

"You was free to run away after they left?"

"Told me to stay put or else, Daddy."

Tucker closed his eyes and leaned his head back against the wall. He kept it there and said: "Noah took your necklace?"

"Uh huh."

"Took your knife too?"

"Yeah."

"Noah warned you to stay put or else?"

"Uh huh."

Tucker lifted his head off the wall and looked directly into his son's eyes. "Noah done all this by himself?"

Travis started to nod and then stopped suddenly, his father's implications finally hitting their mark. Travis dropped his head.

Tucker leaned his head back on the wall again and let out a long, defeated sigh. "Well, if this ain't the fucking boy who cried wolf, I don't know what is."

CHAPTER 56

It was their Sunday tradition. A trip to the cemetery so Ethan and Noah Daigle could visit with their mother and father, and then lunch at a little fry up spot the Daigle boys enjoyed.

Russ Burk had been true to his word and saw that Ron and Adelyn Daigle had received an exceptional service, and the boys were grateful. Though much of Ron and Adelyn had been recovered, a closed casket for each had been the end result.

Russ and Liz were fortunate not to have had such a decision to make for Vicky. Her condition allowed an open casket viewing. The turnout was tremendous. Friends and family—the Daigle boys among them—and the ever-present press who were camped outside the church like gypsies, always desperate for more insight on "The Swamp Slaughters" or "Evil in the Everglades" or a dozen other little titles the media had tried, hopeful one would stick.

Dan's service had been another situation entirely. An empty coffin had been buried.

"Any word on what's gonna happen to Tucker Roy?" Ethan asked out of the blue, french fry halfway to his mouth to suggest indifference to a topic that was anything but. A topic they'd only discussed once since.

Russ and Liz exchanged a little glance. Liz had been staying with her father in Bonita Springs ever since the incident, she pretending to claim she was doing it for her father, he pretending to convince her he would be fine, both pretending that neither one of them was ready to be apart just yet.

"Still pleading guilty to it all," Russ eventually said.

Noah shook his head. "I don't get it. Why would he confess to it all? If it was me, I'd pin it on Harlon and Ida. They're dead; they can't deny nothing."

Russ said: "If it was *you*, you'd be a psycho getting a free lunch right now."

They all laughed.

"Noah's got a point though. Why *would* Tucker cop to it all? The state'll fry him," Ethan said.

"Who knows?" Liz said. "Guilt maybe?"

"For killing Mama and Daddy?" Noah asked.

"For all of it," Liz said. "When it was all said and done, the whole thing did boil down to a stupid little lie."

"You think Tucker found out Travis lied?"

"Maybe," Liz said. "Maybe confessing—facing certain punishment—is his way of putting things right. Reparations."

"What does that mean?" Noah asked.

"She just said, dummy," Ethan said. "It means putting things right."

"Be nice," Russ said.

"Still doesn't make any sense to me," Noah said. "You think he'd wanna stay free and look after Travis. Y'all said he made a fuss to Harlon and Ida about going out and looking for him when he thought we had him tied up."

Liz shrugged. "Well, maybe in the end, he felt having to see Travis every day would be too much to handle. A constant reminder that his wife and baby were dead because of his son's lies."

"So you *do* think Tucker found out Travis was lying? That's why he confessed?" Noah asked.

"If I had to guess, I'd say yes. But who knows? If this ordeal has taught me anything, it's that there are some really fucked up people in this world."

Both Ethan and Noah burst out laughing.

Russ bit back a smile and nudged his daughter. "Language!"

When the laughter died, they ate in silence for a few minutes. And then it was Liz's turn to ask a question. "So, have you seen Travis in school?"

Noah shook his head. "I heard he moved away."

"Who's he staying with?" Russ asked.

Noah shrugged. "Don't know. The boogeyman, I hope."

Ethan chuckled.

"So, you think two wrongs make a right?" Russ asked with a curious eye, a mentoring moment maybe.

Noah—always polite, always respectful—could not help but glare at Russ. "We never *did* anything wrong."

Every Sunday after lunch, Russ would offer to take the boys back to Bonita Springs to go swimming, and every Sunday the boys would politely decline.

Today they agreed. And they got to Russ' place and their eyes popped and their jaws dropped...and they fell asleep by the pool.

THE END

ABOUT THE AUTHOR

A Philadelphia area native, Jeff has published multiple works, both fiction and nonfiction. In 2011 he received the Red Adept Reviews Indie Award for Horror.

Jeff is most notable for his bestselling *Bad Games* books. Currently, all three *Bad Games* books are being optioned for feature films, and are available individually or altogether in one complete box set.

Hair of the Bitch, another of Jeff's novels catering to dark thriller fans, was hailed as one of the best novels of 2014 by bestselling author and Bram Stoker Award nominee John Dixon.

Free time is spent reading, watching mixed martial arts, horror films and The Three Stooges, and paying more attention to animals than people. He is determined to pet (and maybe cuddle) a lion one day.

Jeff loves to hear from his readers. Please feel free to contact him to discuss anything and everything. Be sure to sign up and leave your email address (don't worry, Jeff hates spam as much as he does spiders) for occasional updates on all future works!

info@jeffmenapace.com

http://jeffmenapace.com/books/

Connect with Jeff on Facebook and Twitter:

www.facebook.com/JeffMenapace.writer

http://twitter.com/JeffMenapace

OTHER WORKS
BY JEFF MENAPACE

Please visit Jeff's Amazon Author Page, or his website for a complete list of all available works!

http://www.amazon.com/Jeff-Menapace/e/B004R09M0S

www.jeffmenapace.com

AUTHOR'S NOTE:

Thank you so much for taking the time to read *Wildlife*. Every single reader is important to me. Whenever I'm asked what my writing goals are, my number one answer, without pause, is to entertain.

I want you to have fun reading what I write. I want to make your heart race. I want you to get paper cuts (or Kindle thumb?) from turning the pages so fast. Again—I want to entertain you.

If I succeeded in doing that, I would be very grateful if you took a few minutes to write a review on Amazon for *Wildlife*. Good reviews can be very helpful, and I absolutely love to read the various insights from satisfied readers.

Thank you so very much, my friends. Until next time...

Jeff Menapace

Made in the USA
Las Vegas, NV
30 March 2022